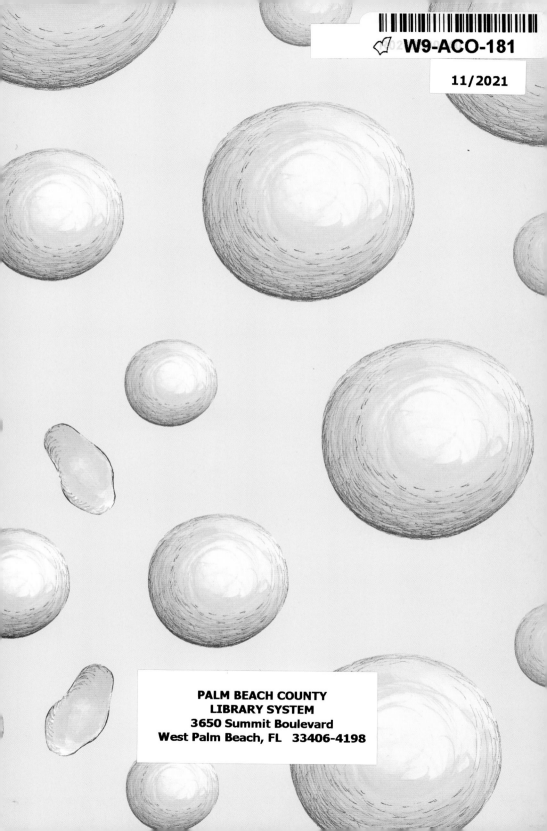

Frog and Ball

KATHY CAPLE

HOLIDAY HOUSE · NEW YORK

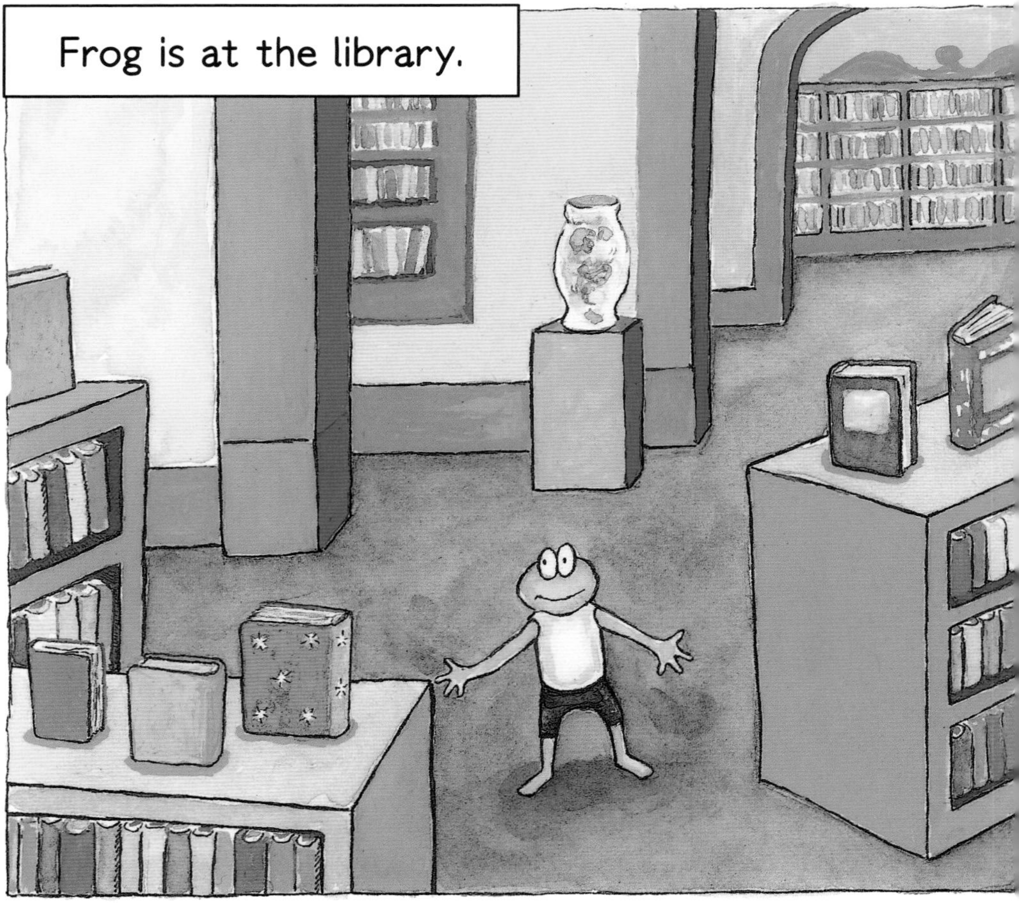
Frog is at the library.

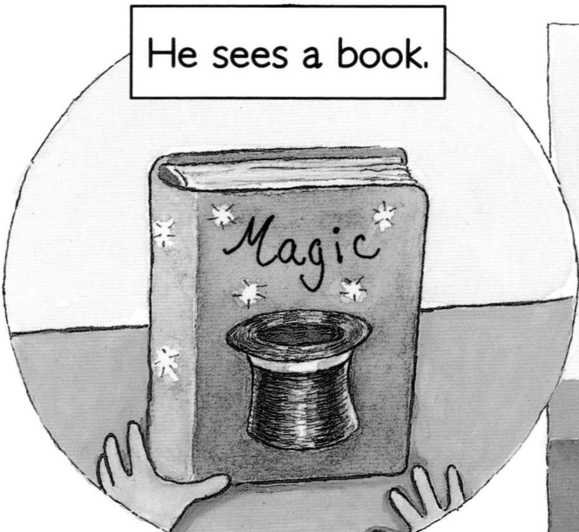
He sees a book.
Magic

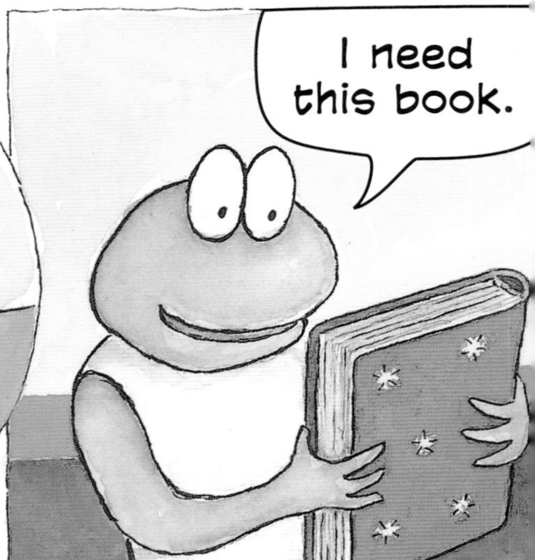
I need this book.

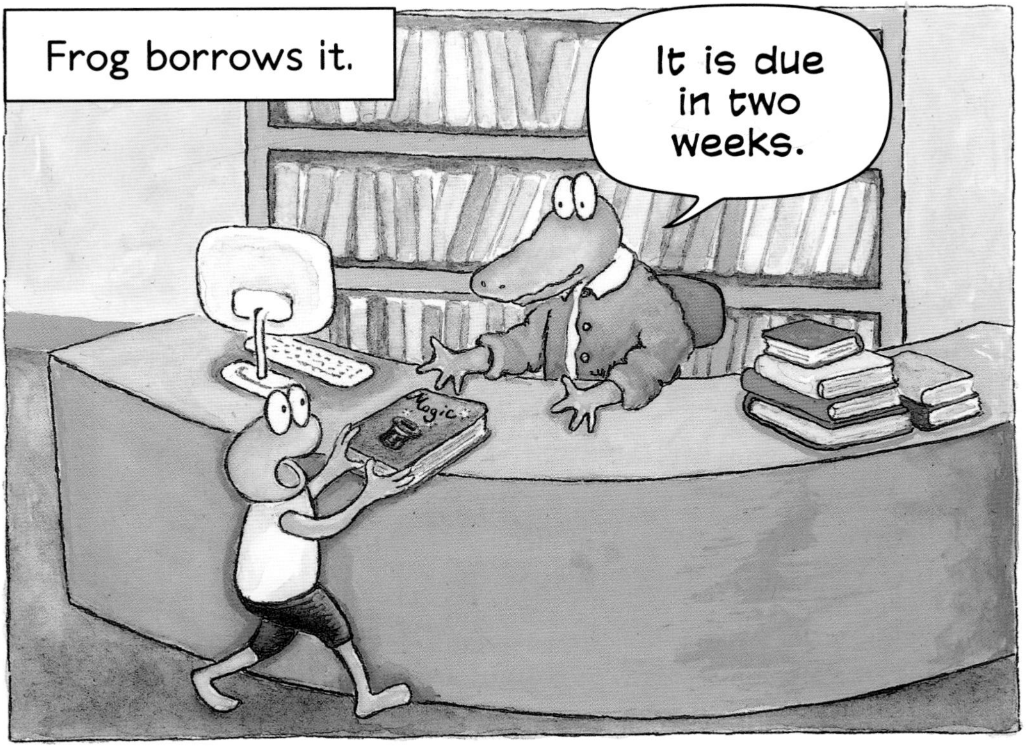
Frog borrows it.
It is due in two weeks.
Magic

He takes the book to the park.

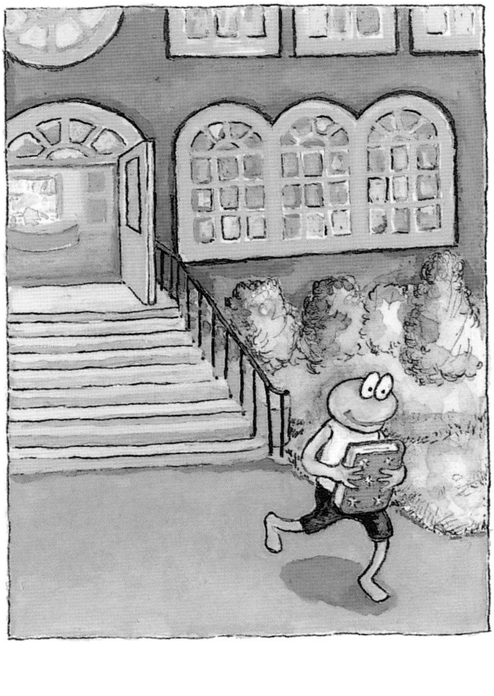

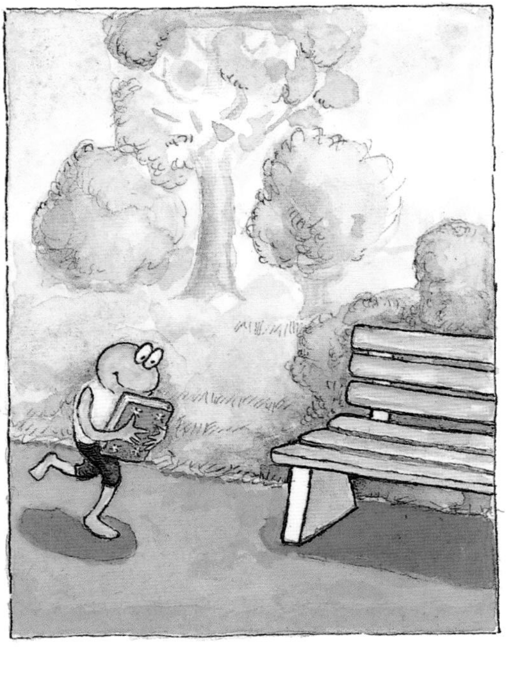

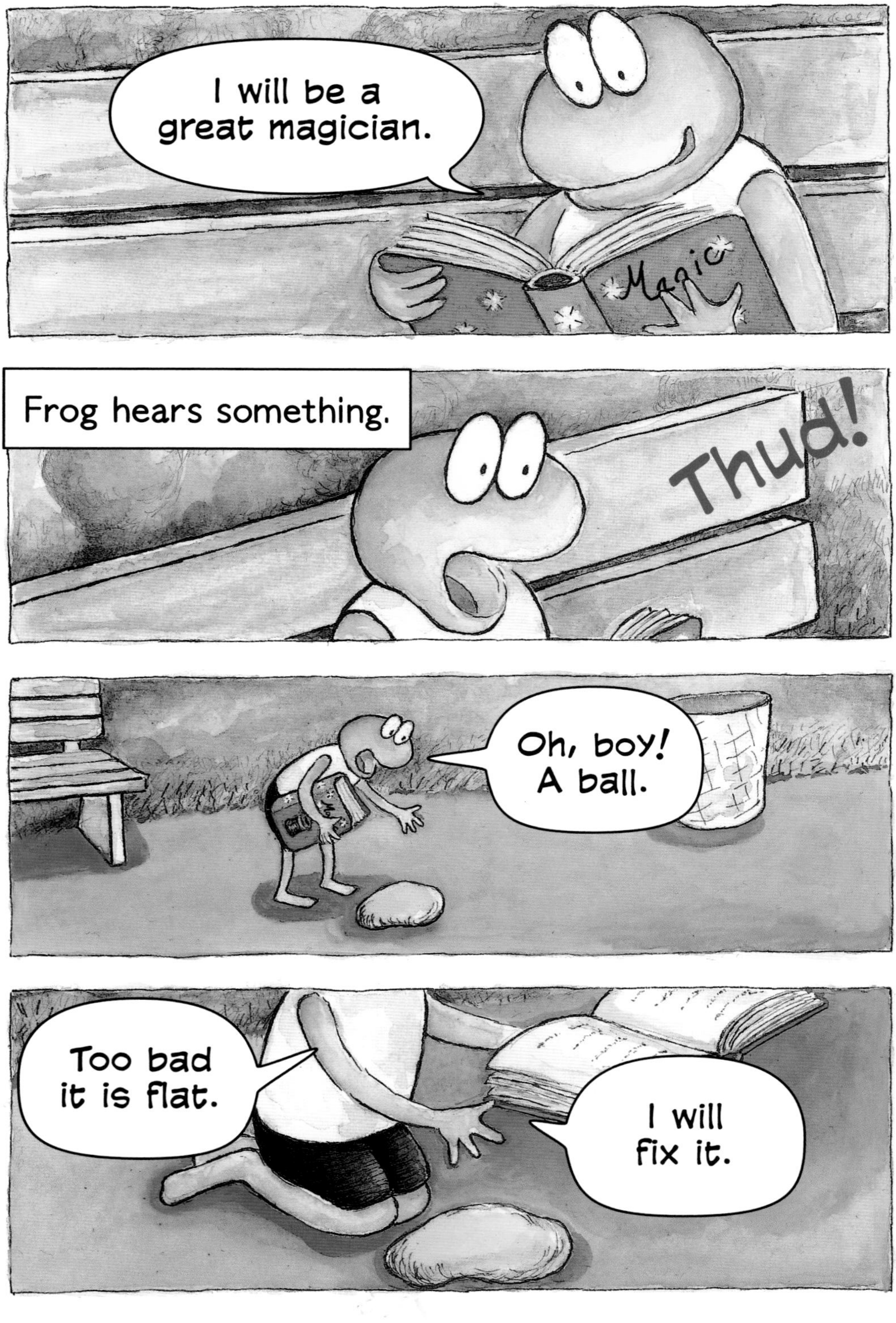
I will be a great magician.
Magic
Frog hears something.
Thud!
Oh, boy! A ball.
Too bad it is flat.
I will fix it.

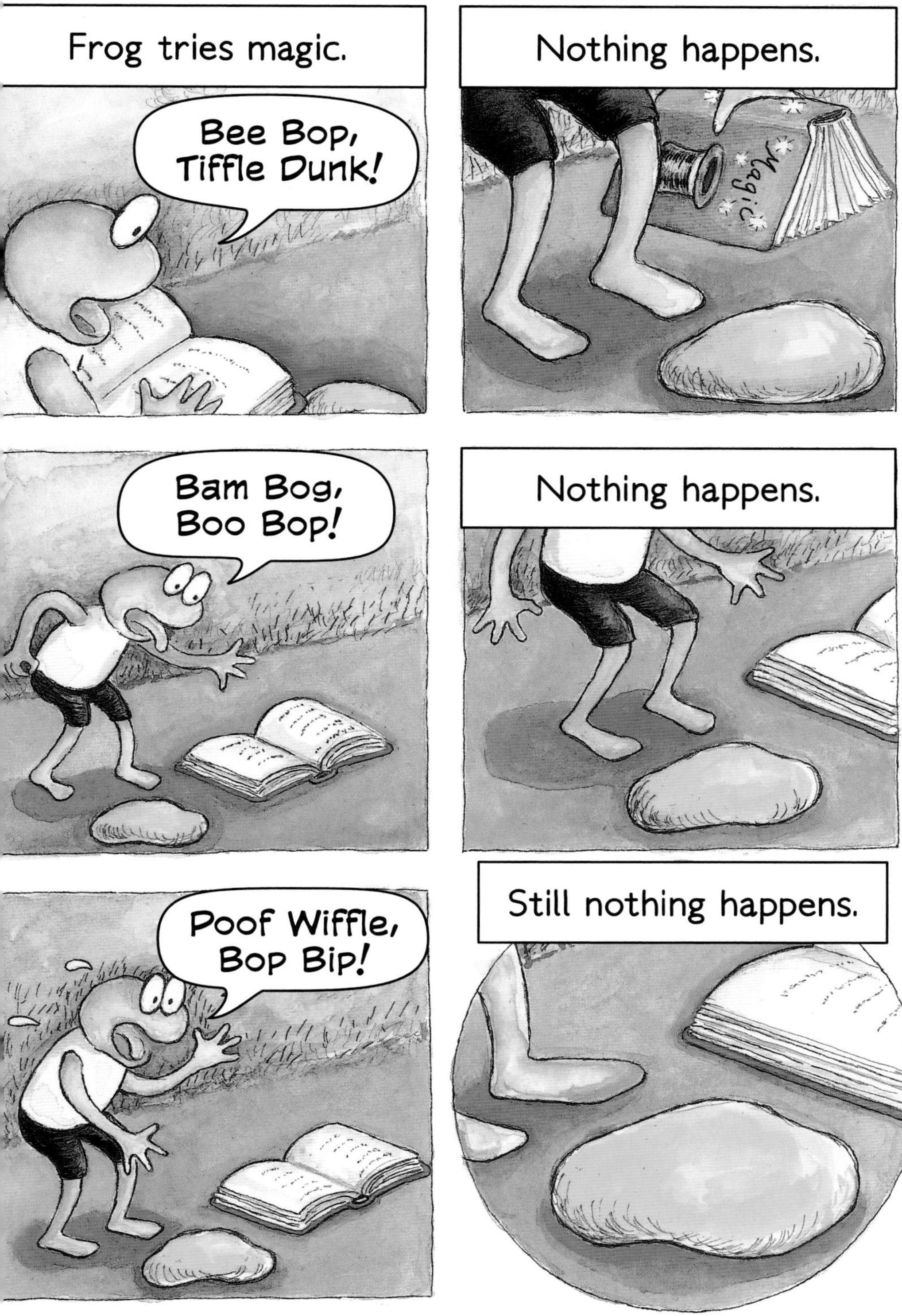
Frog tries magic.
Bee Bop, Tiffle Dunk!
Nothing happens.
Magic
Bam Bog, Boo Bop!
Nothing happens.
Poof Wiffle, Bop Bip!
Still nothing happens.

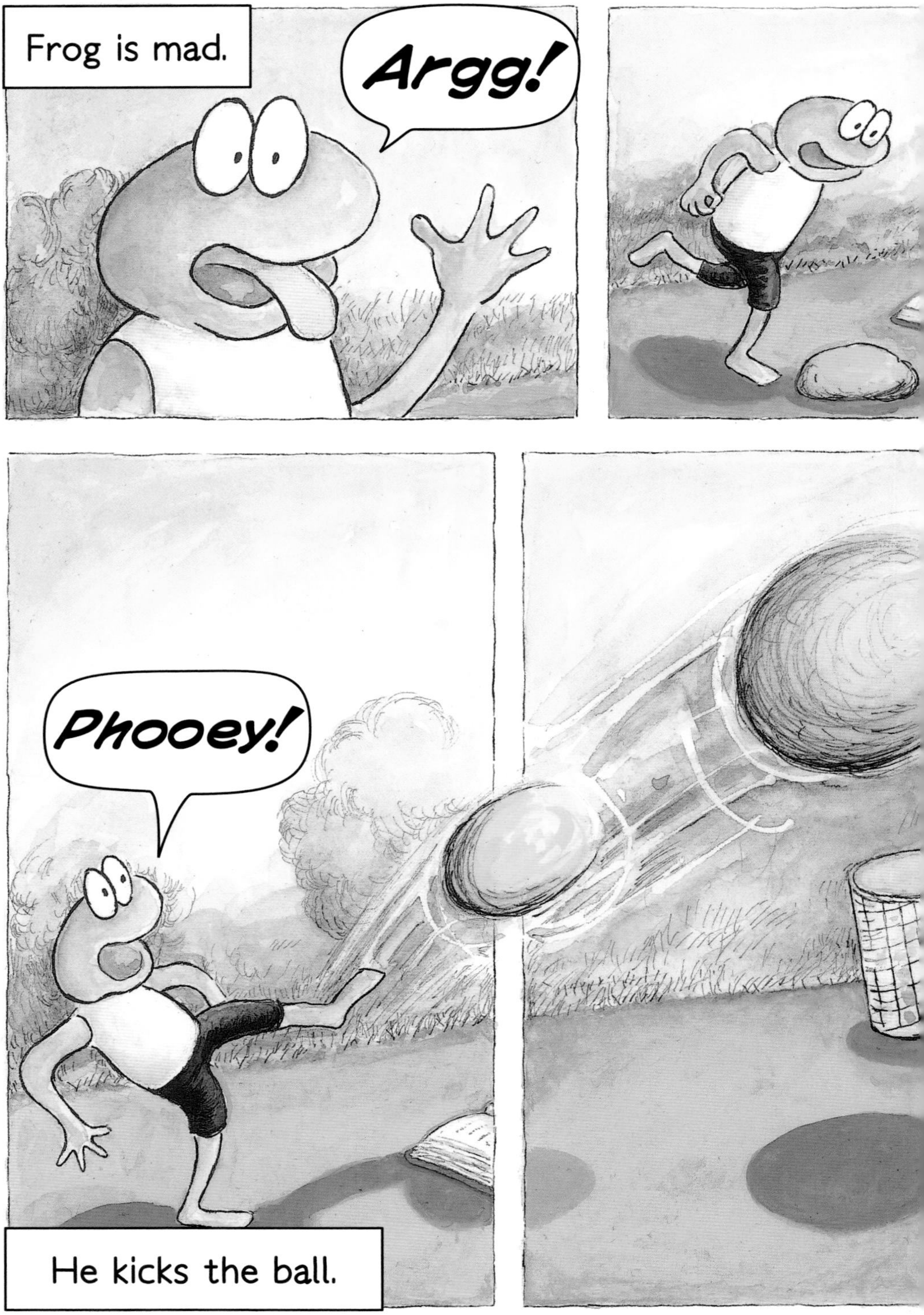
Frog is mad.
Argg!
Phooey!
He kicks the ball.

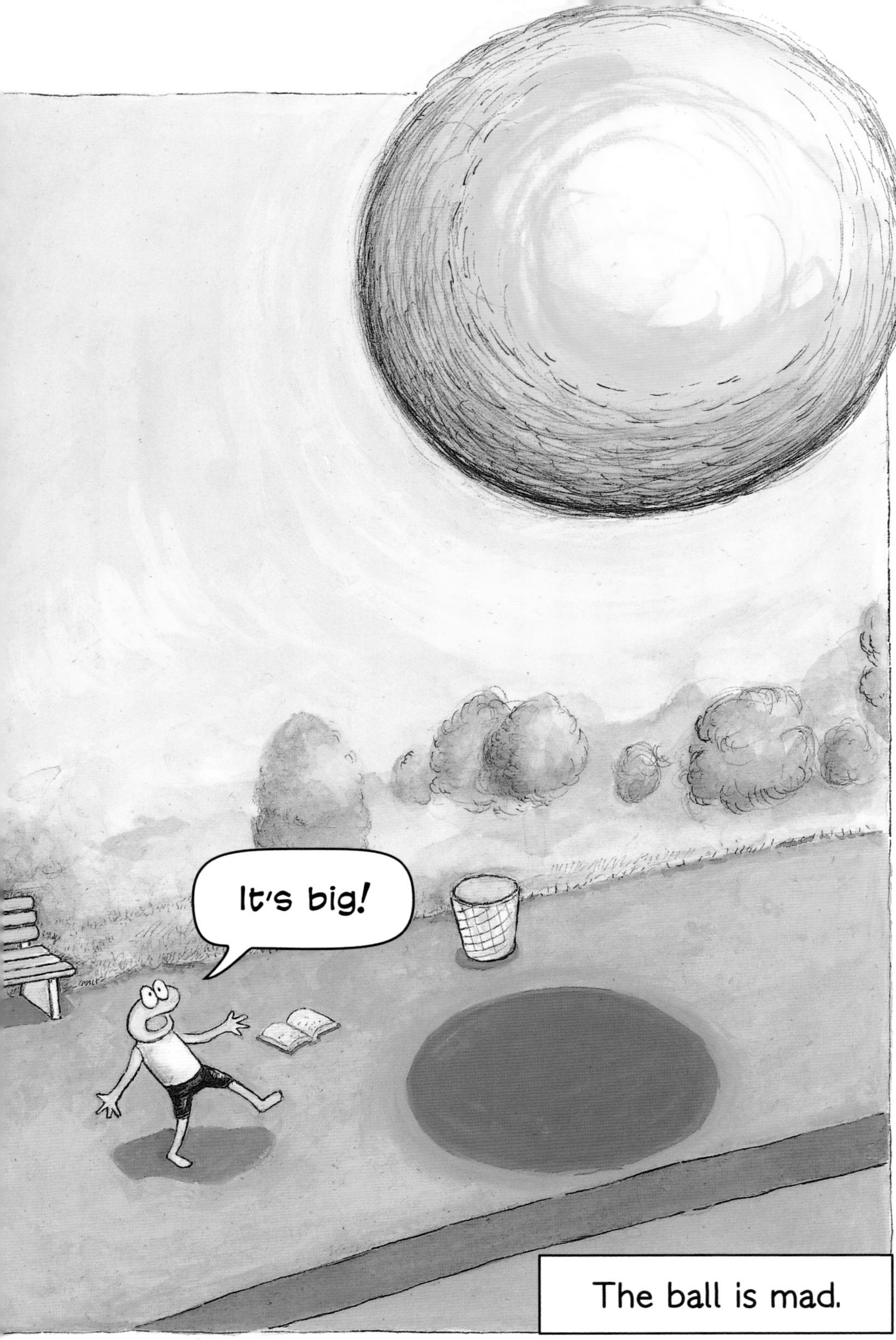
It's big!

The ball is mad.

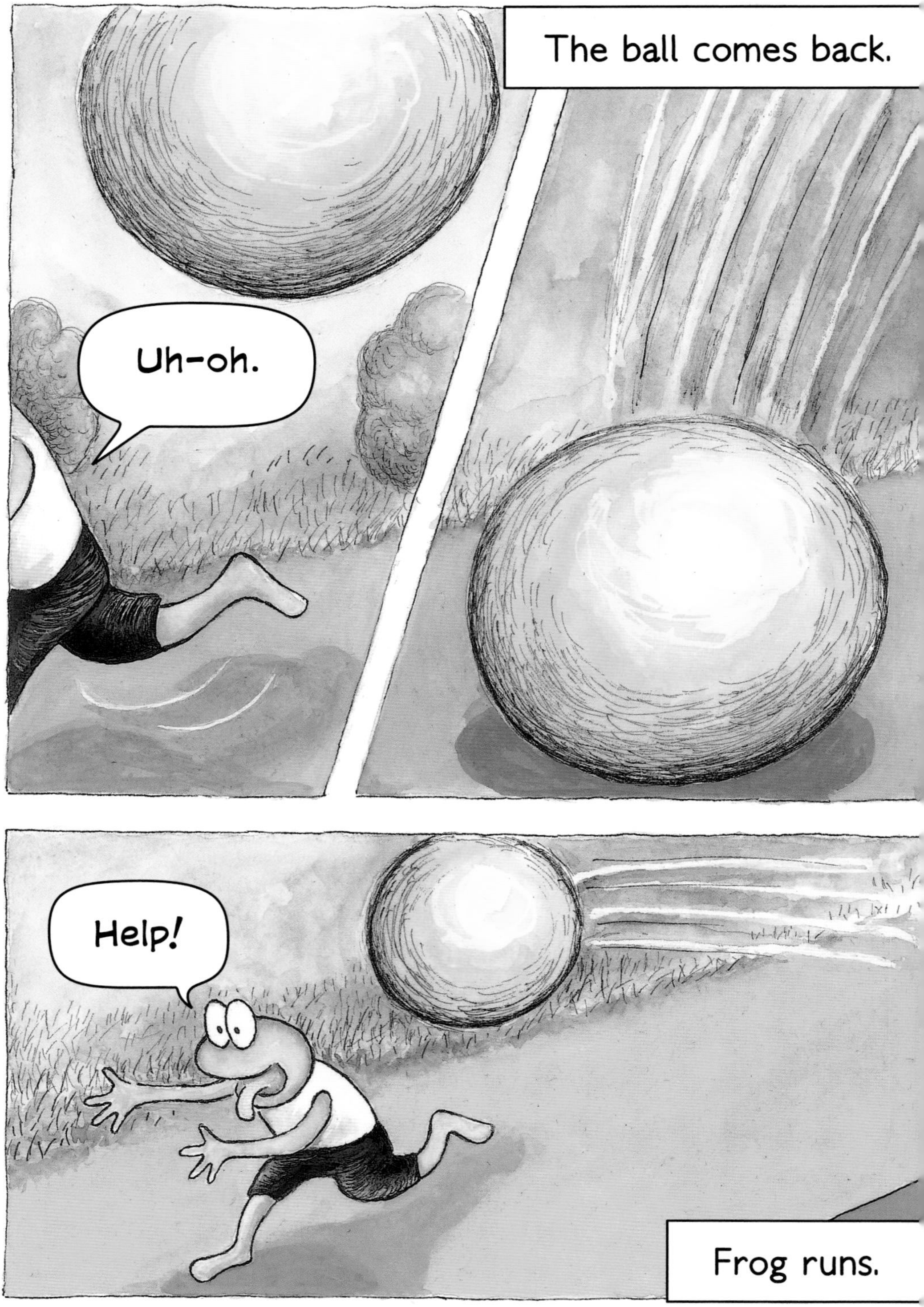
The ball comes back.
Uh-oh.
Help!
Frog runs.

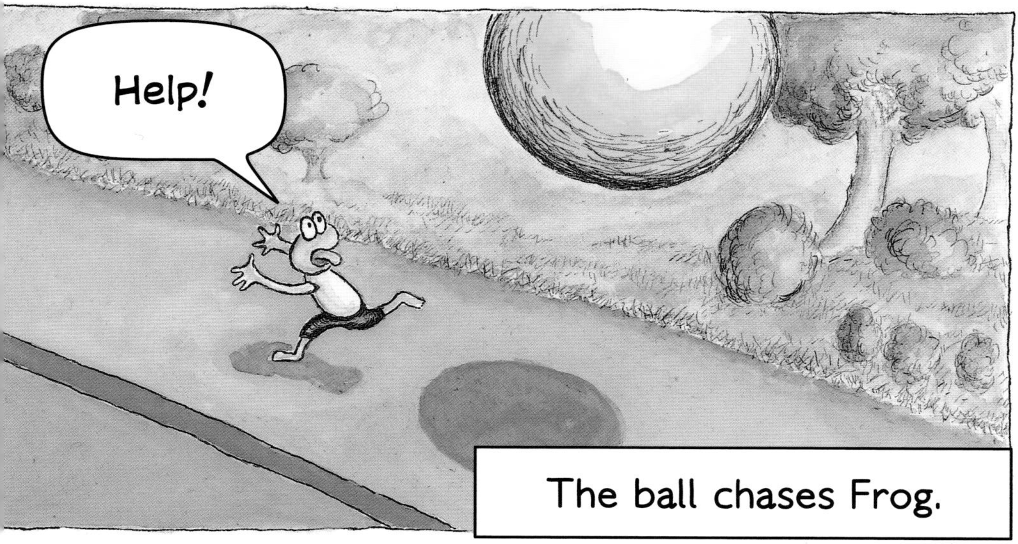
Help!
The ball chases Frog.

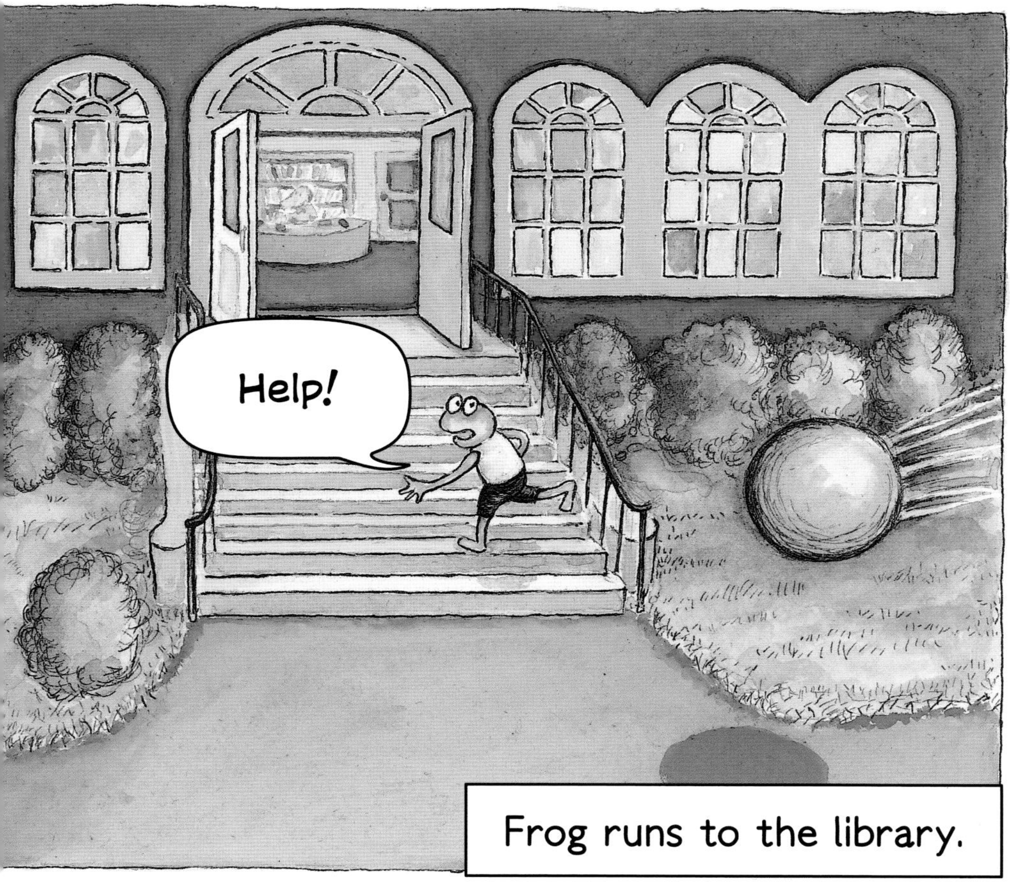
Help!
Frog runs to the library.

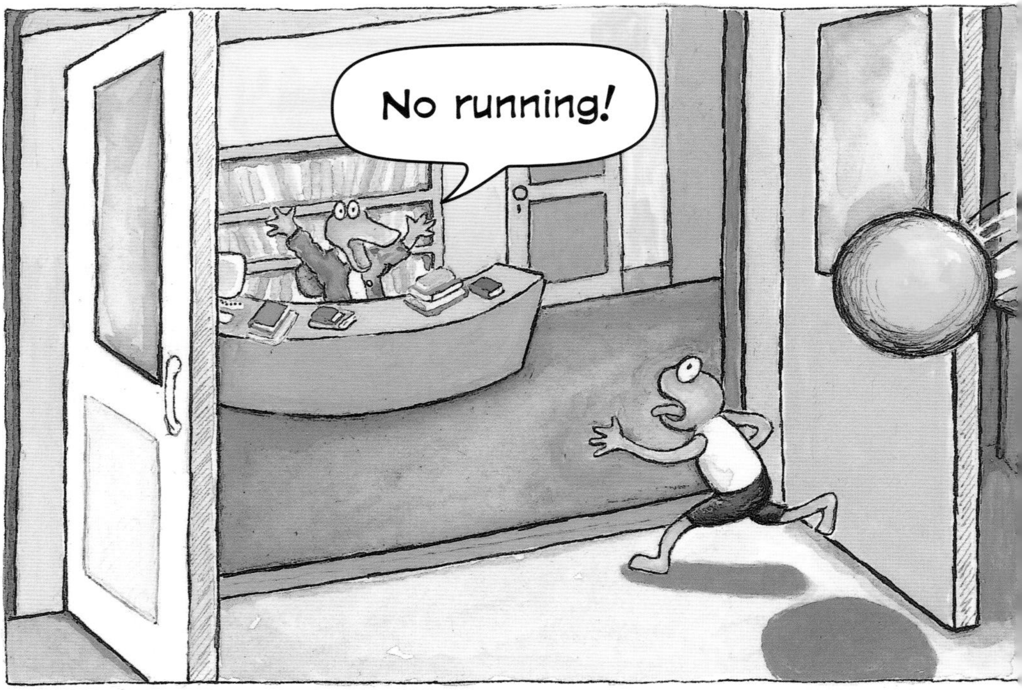
No running!

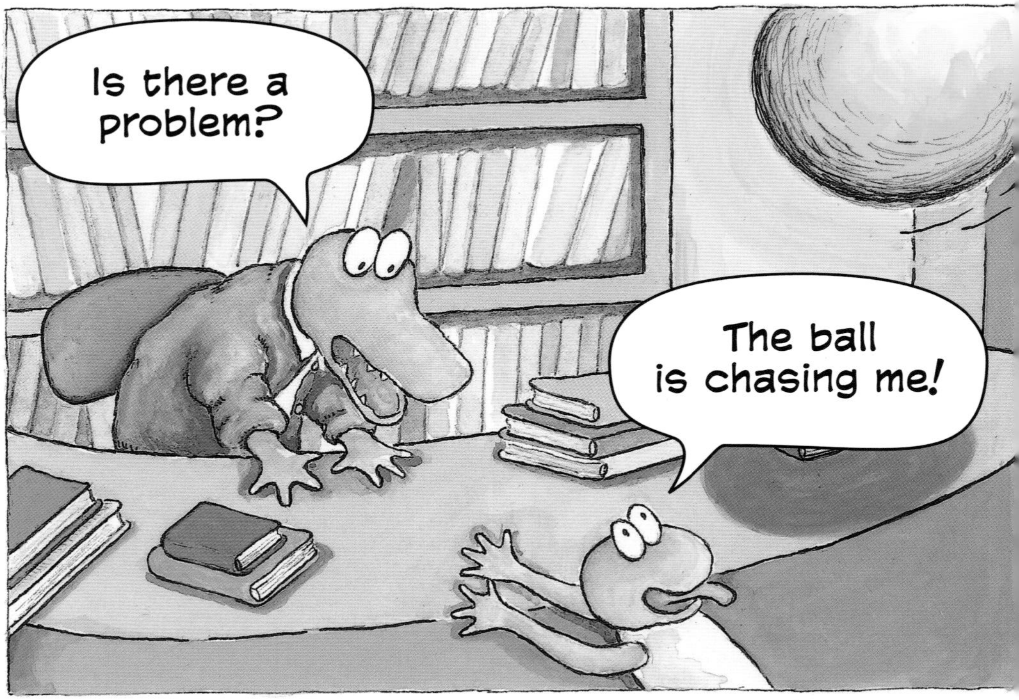
Is there a problem?
The ball is chasing me!

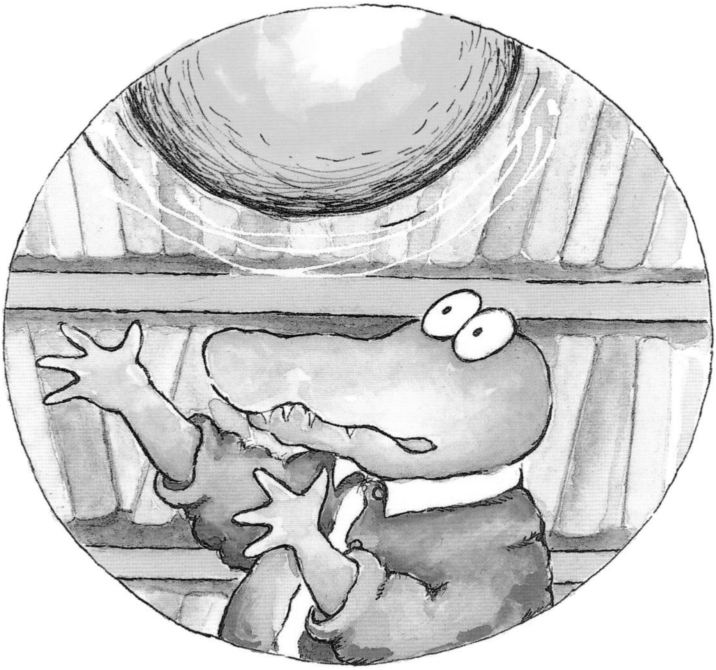

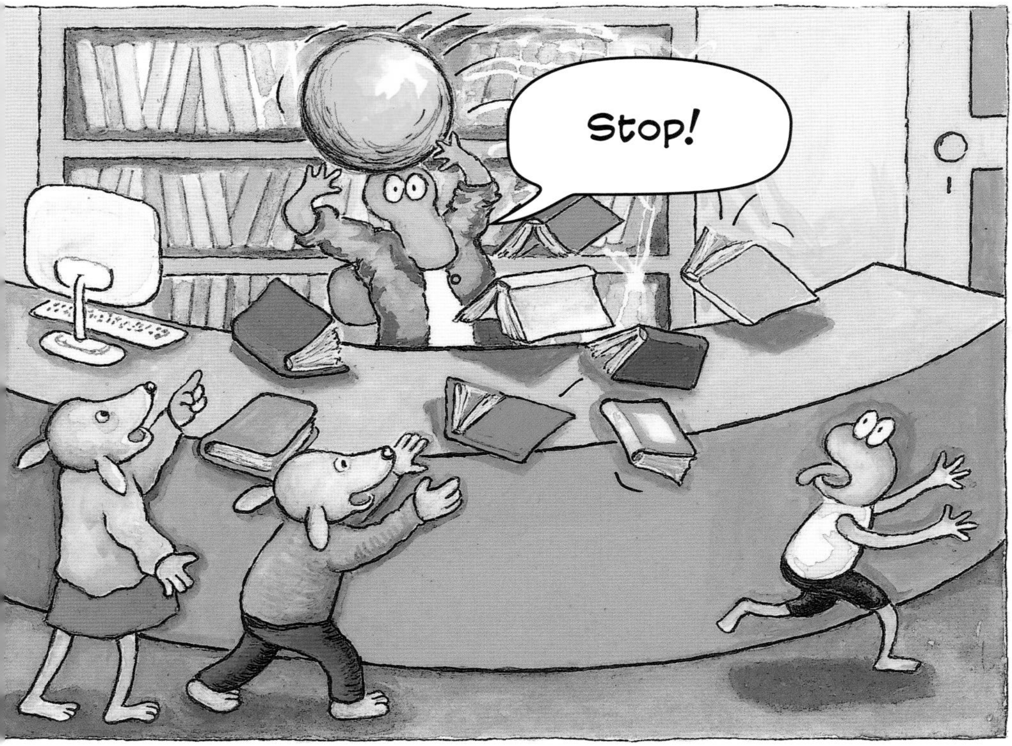
Stop!

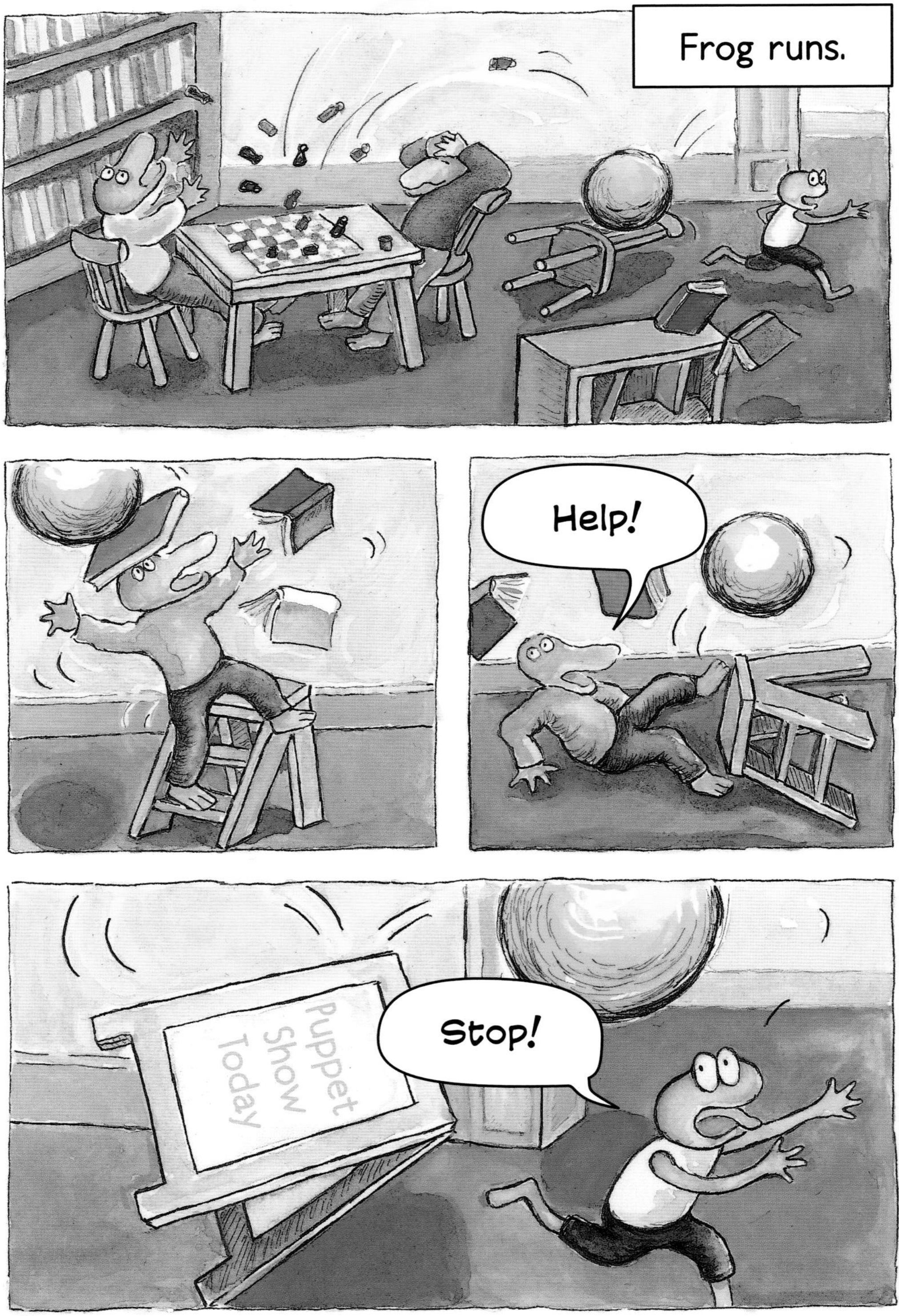
Frog runs.
Help!
Puppet Show Today
Stop!

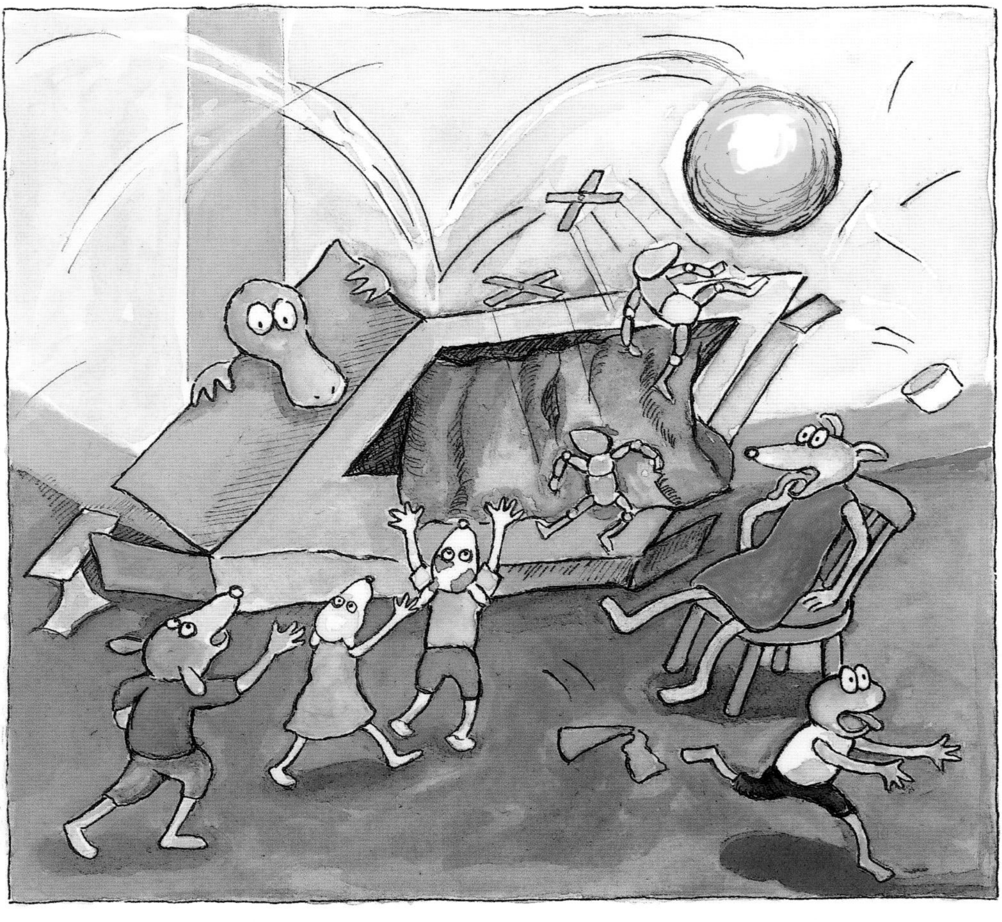

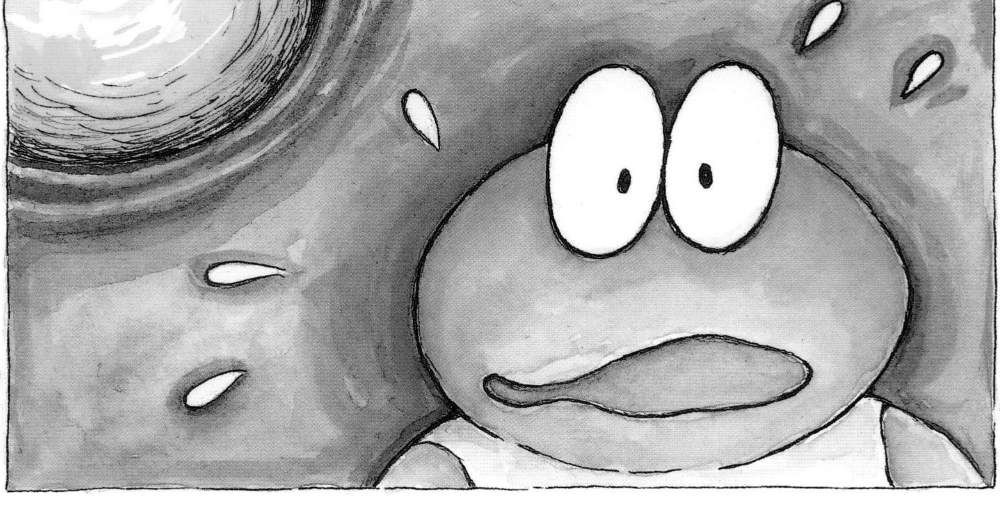

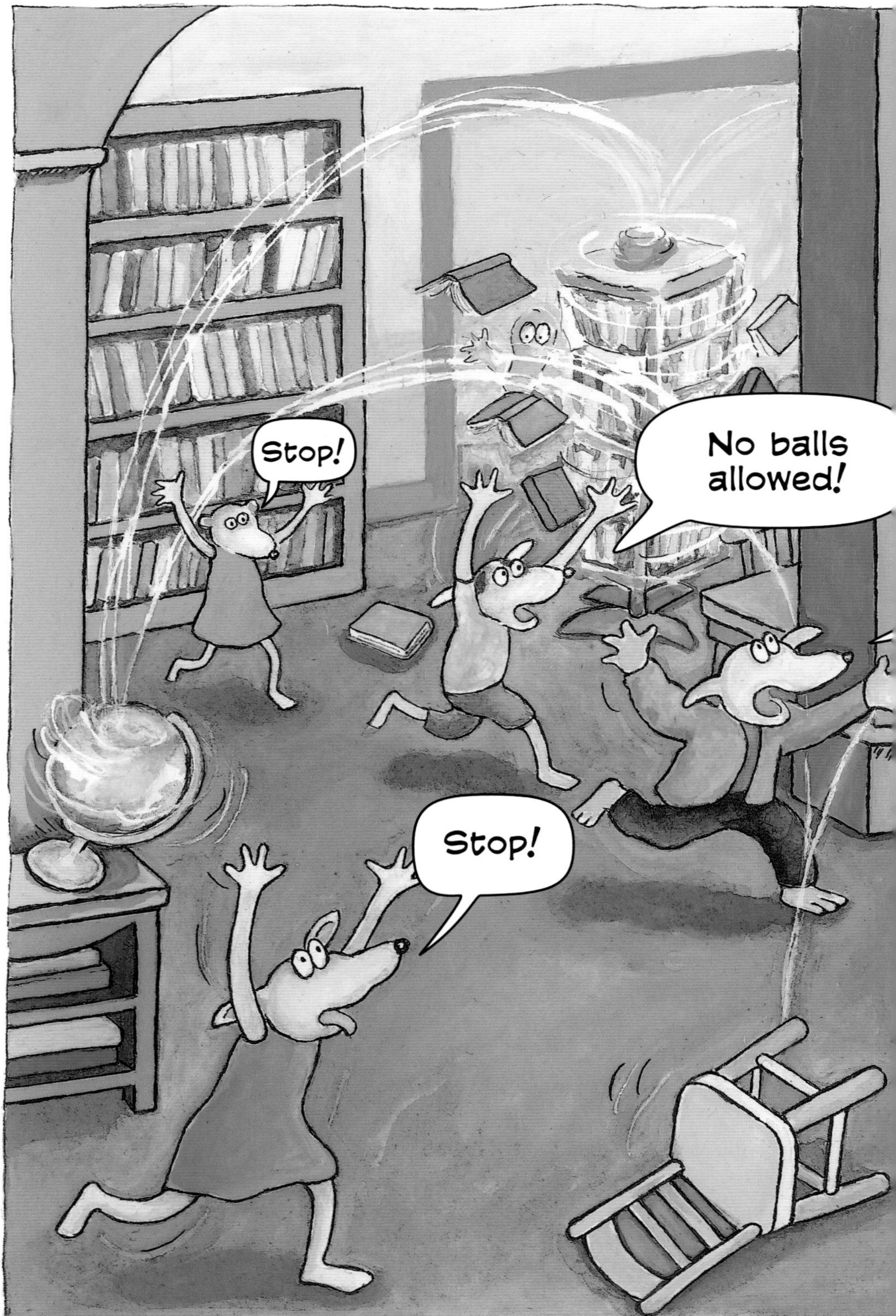
Stop!
No balls allowed!
Stop!

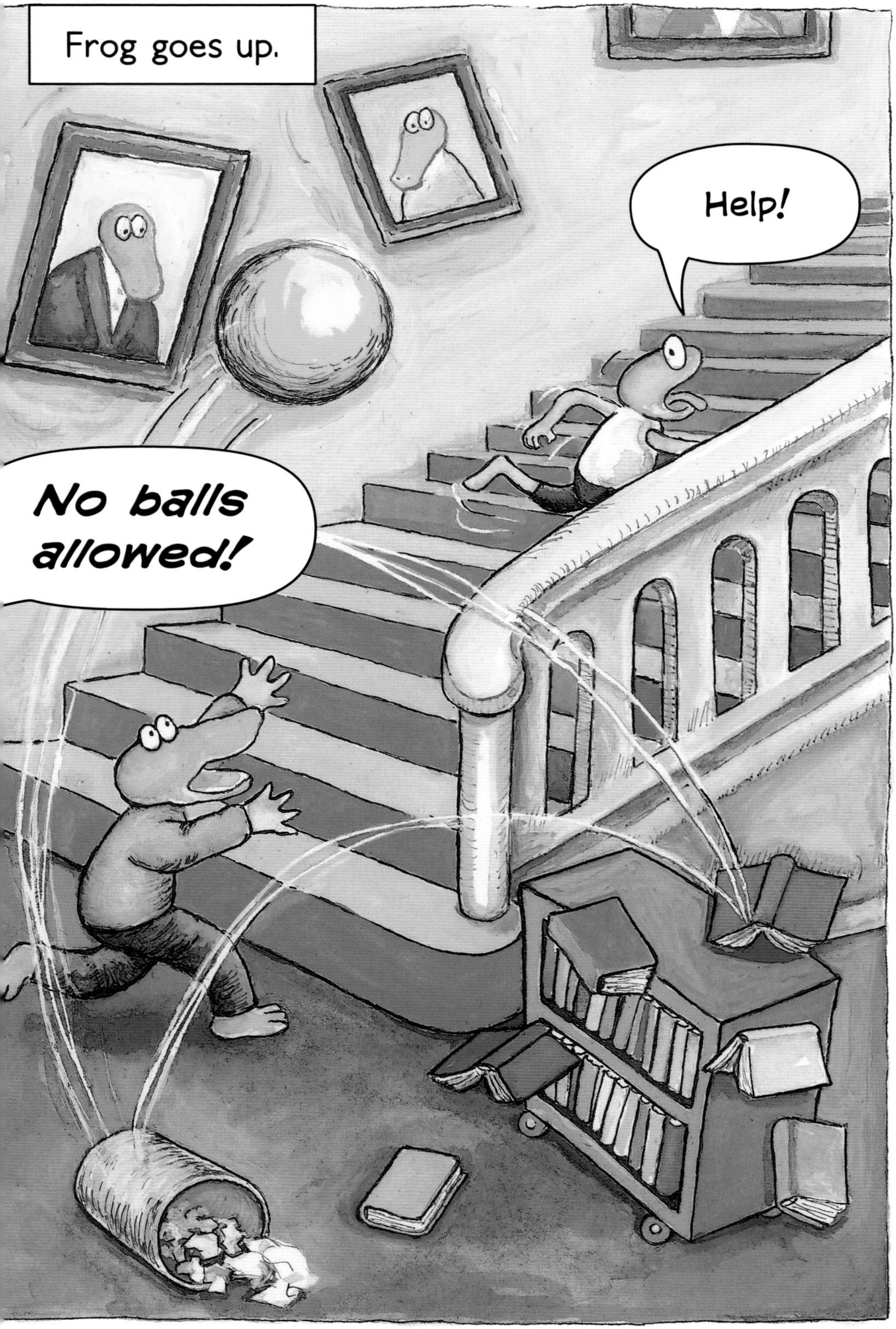
Frog goes up.
Help!
No balls allowed!

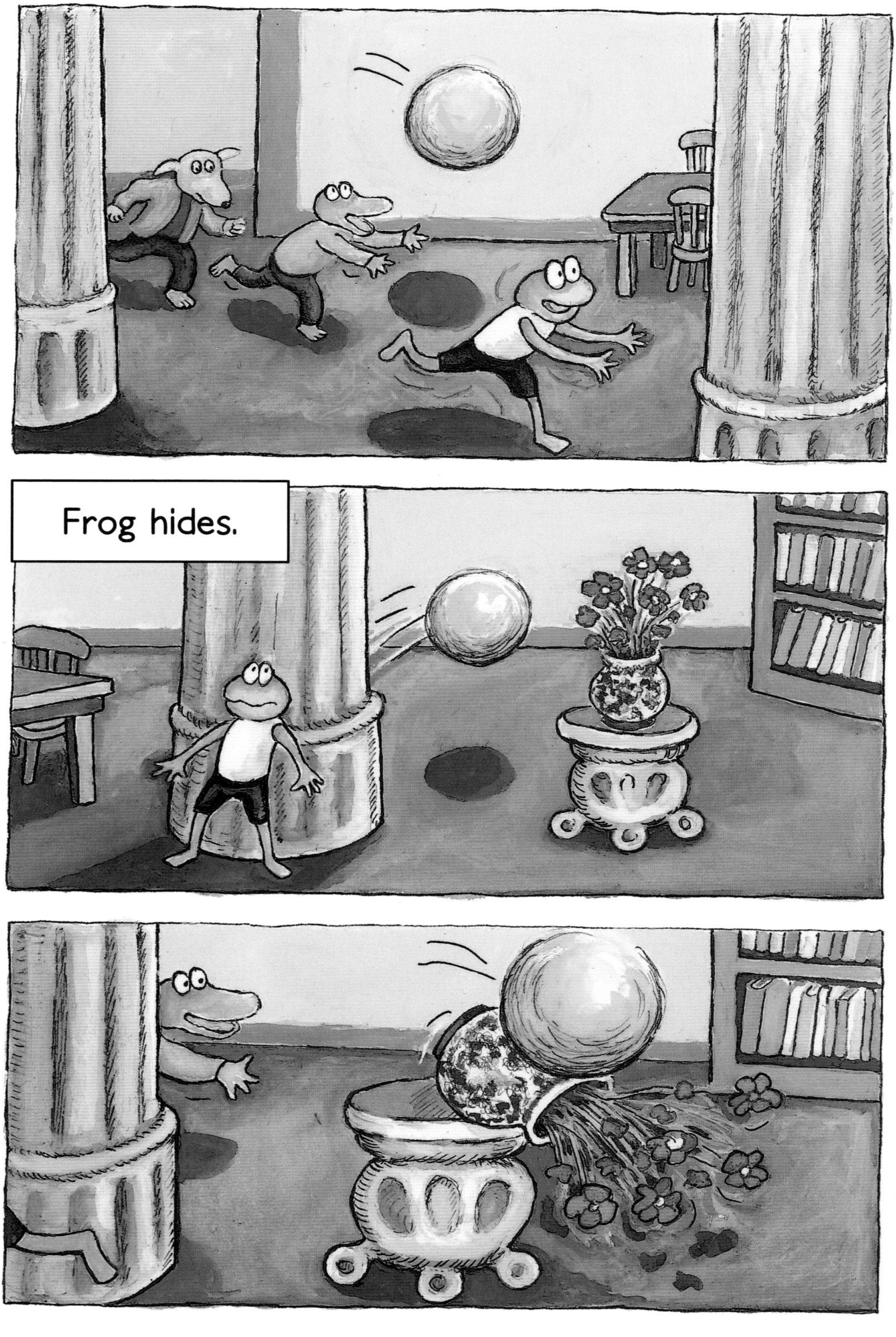
Frog hides.

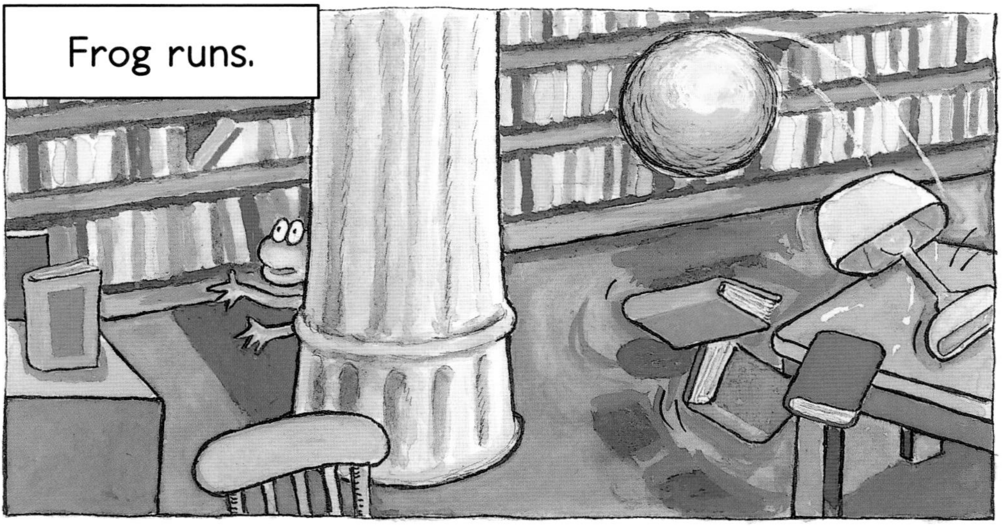
Frog runs.

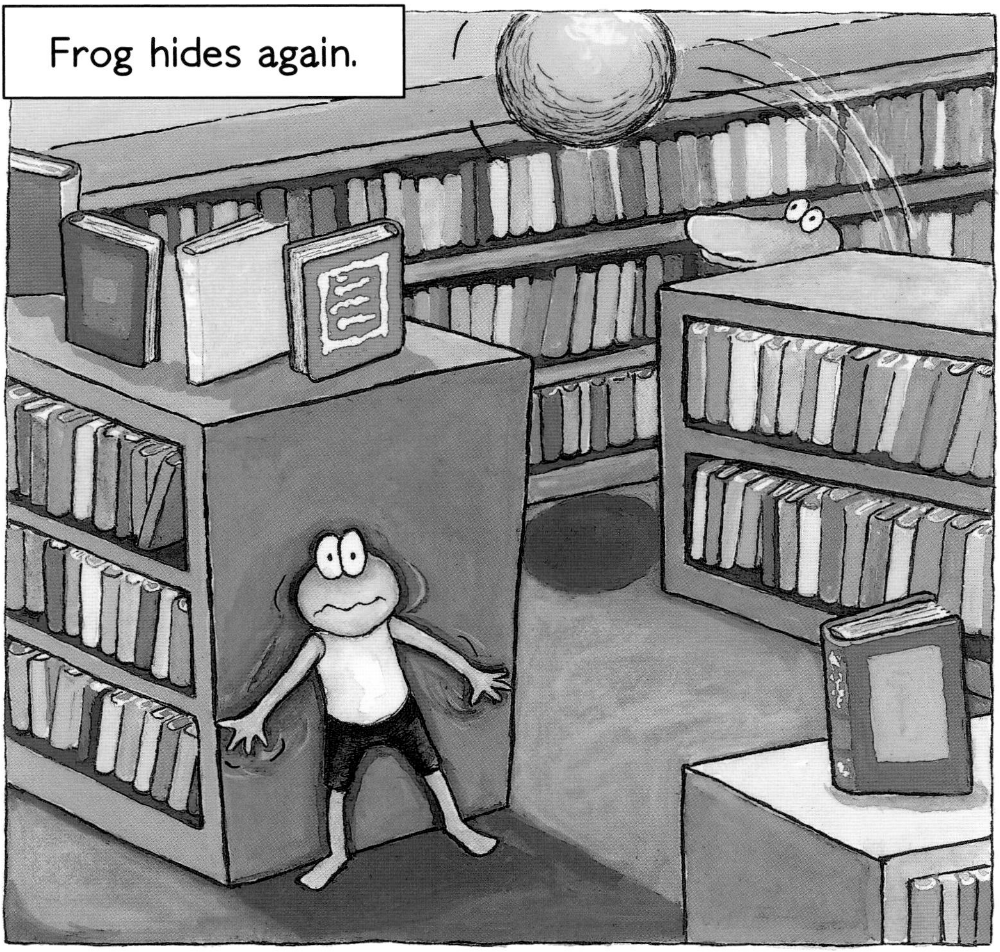
Frog hides again.

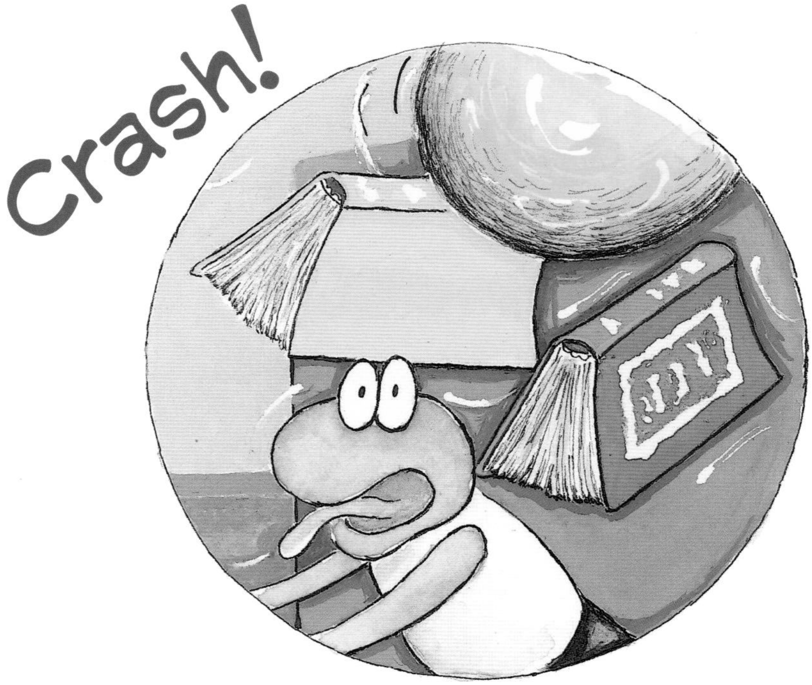
Crash!

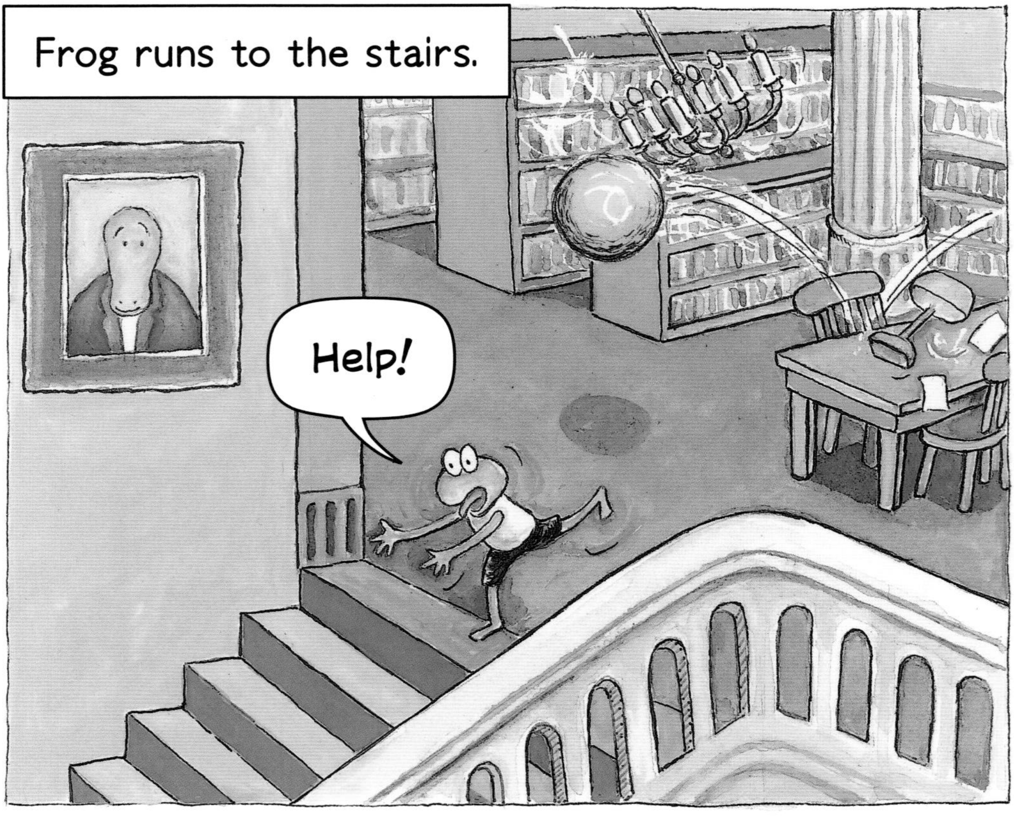
Frog runs to the stairs.
Help!

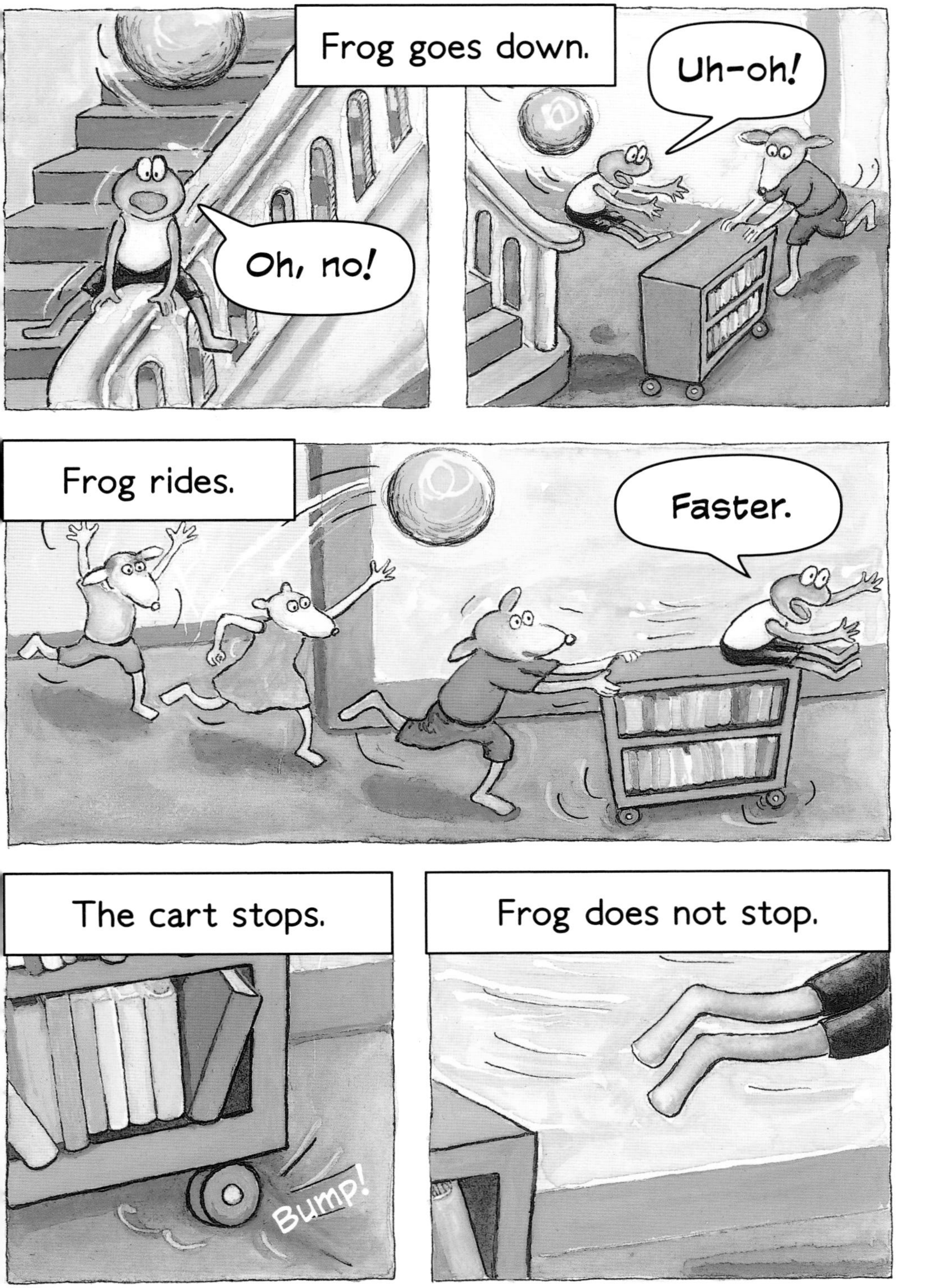
Frog goes down.
Oh, no!
Uh-oh!
Frog rides.
Faster.
The cart stops.
Bump!
Frog does not stop.

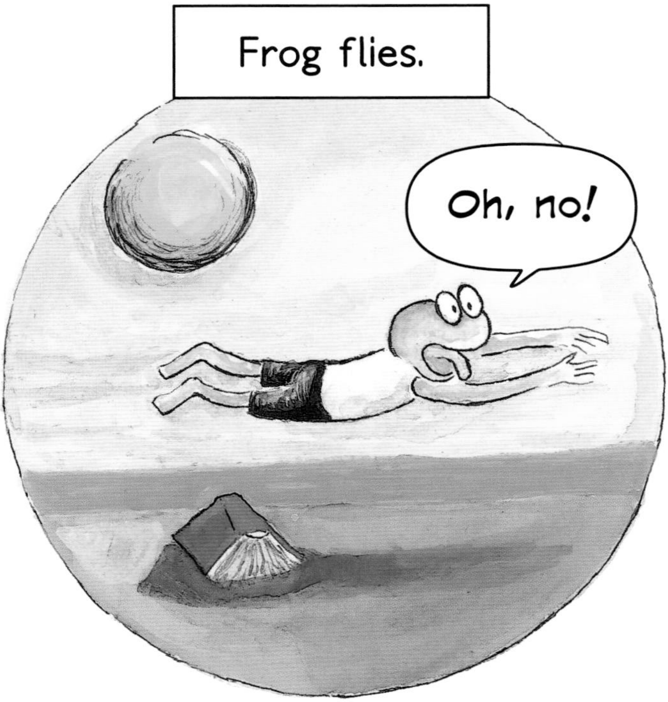
Frog flies.
Oh, no!

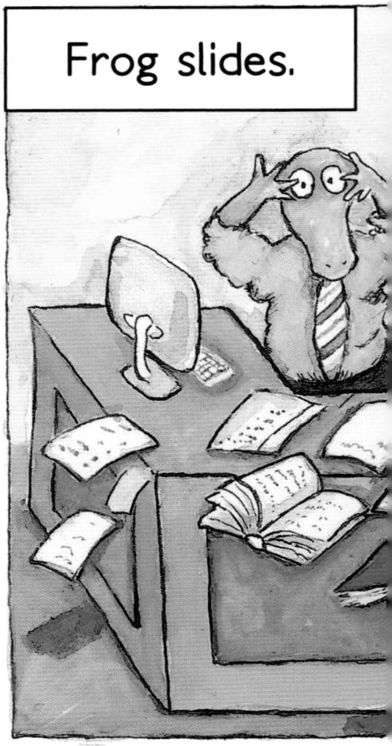
Frog slides.

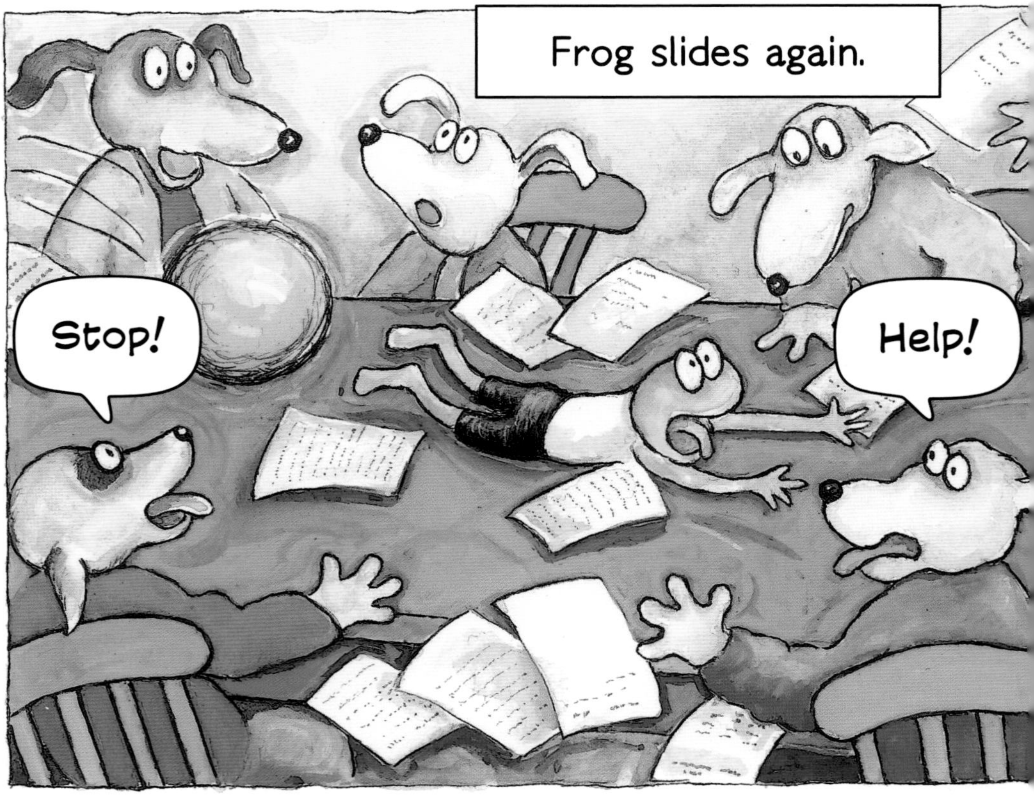
Frog slides again.
Stop!
Help!

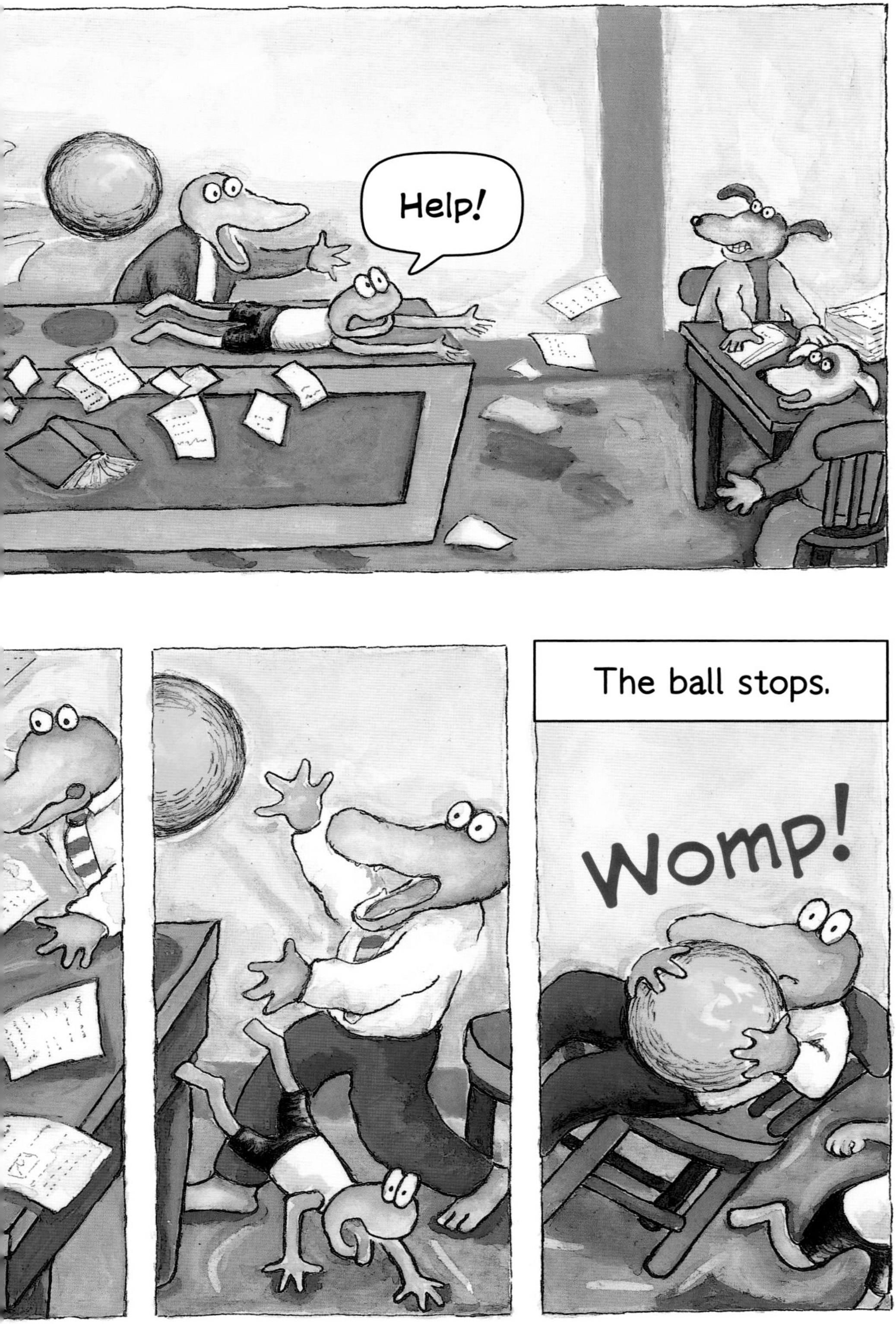
Help!
The ball stops.
Womp!

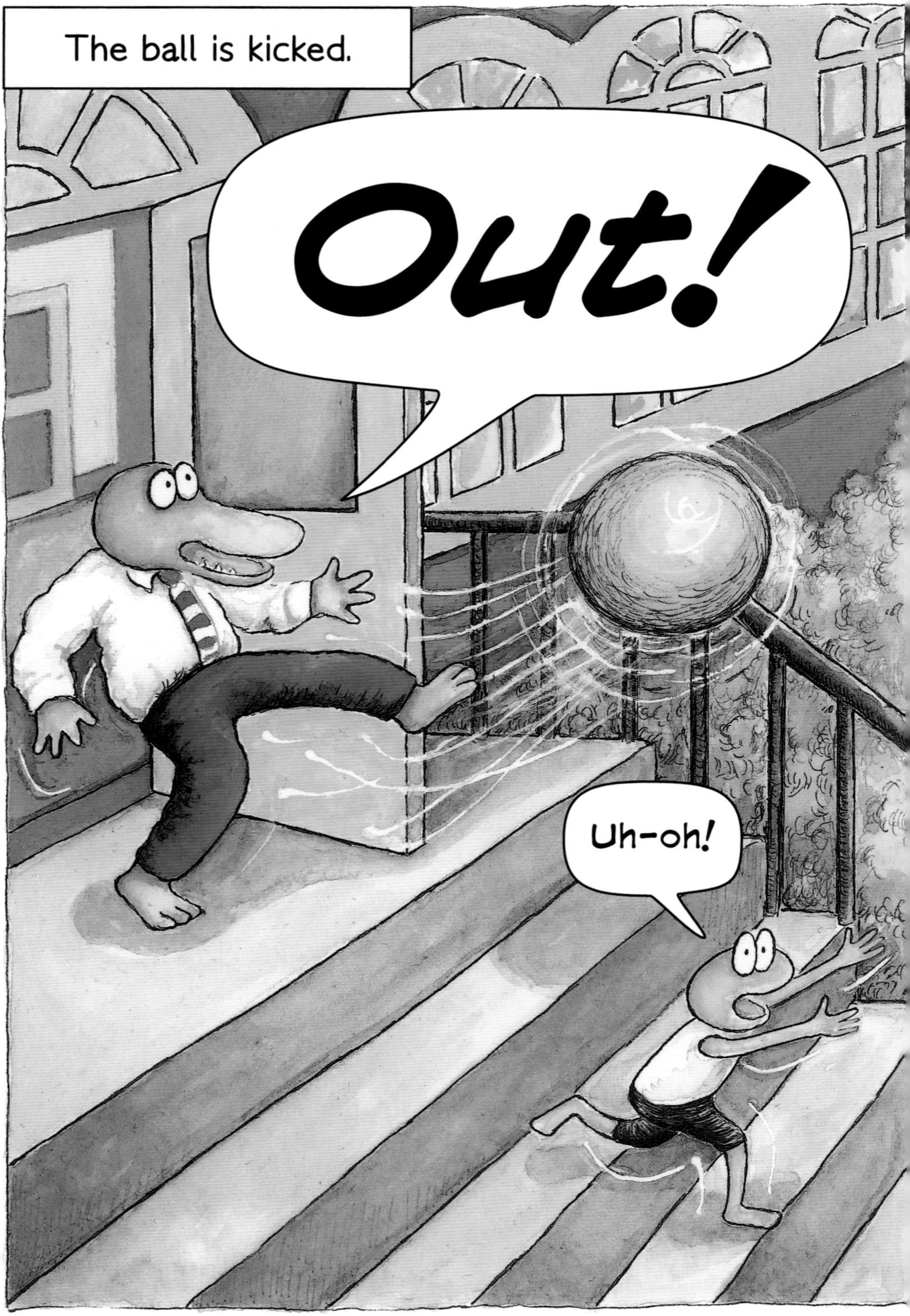
The ball is kicked.
Out!
Uh-oh!

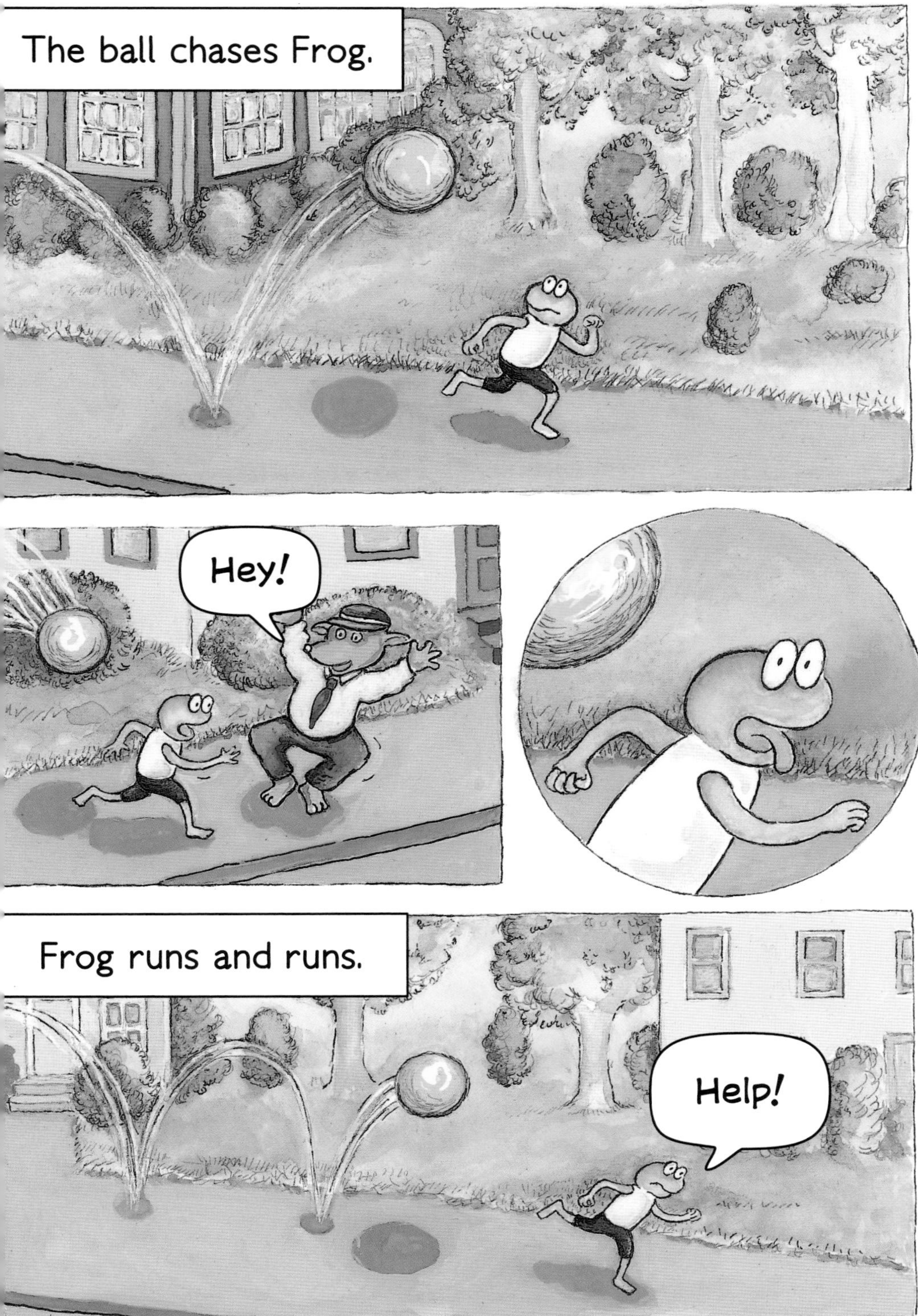
The ball chases Frog.
Hey!
Frog runs and runs.
Help!

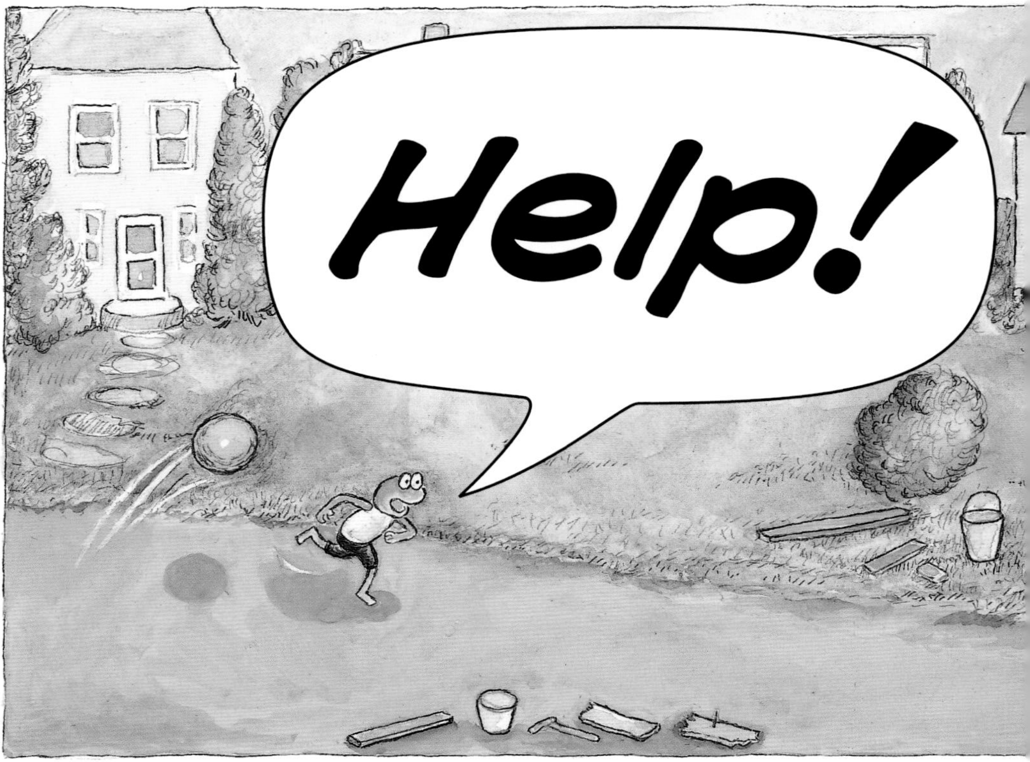
Help!

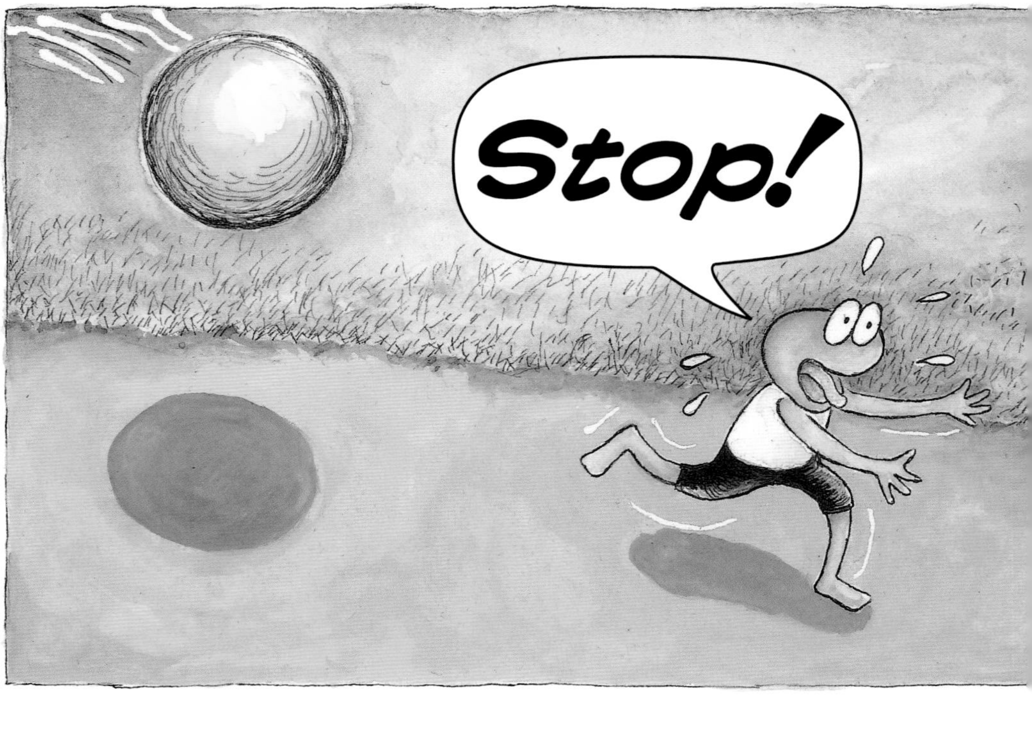
Stop!

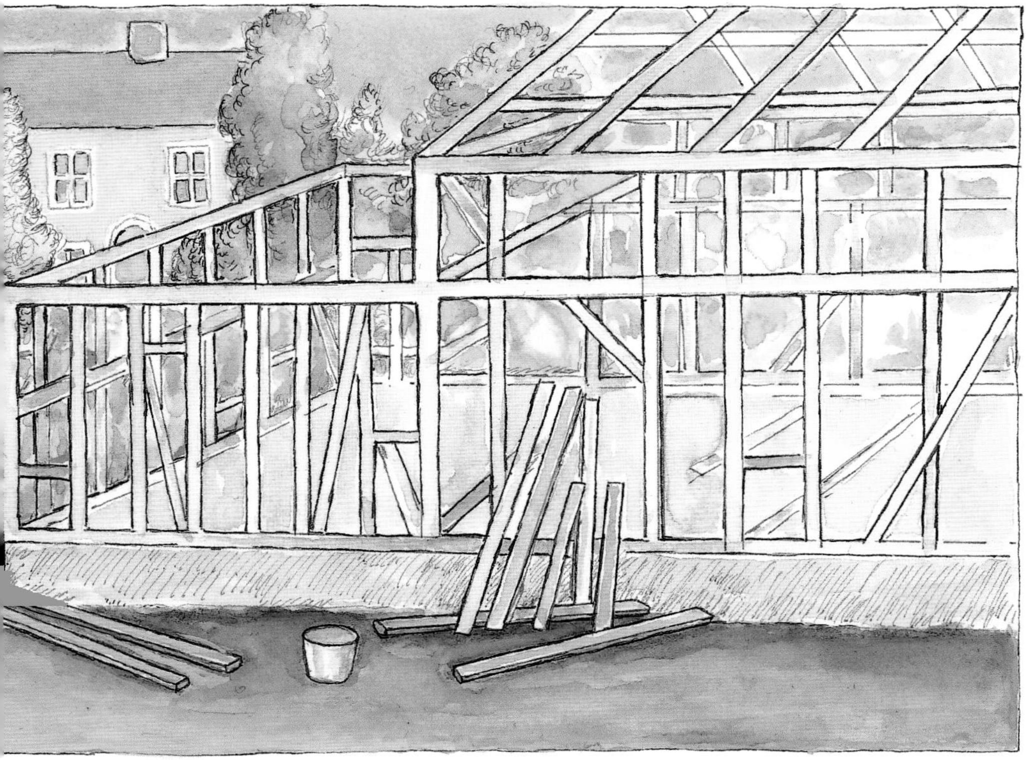

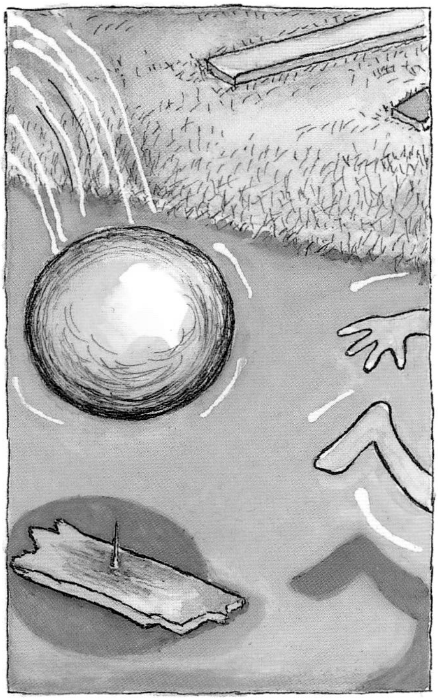

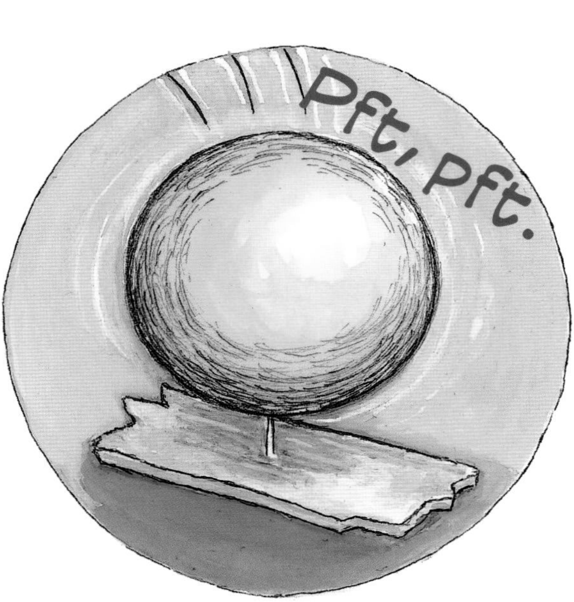
Pft, pft.

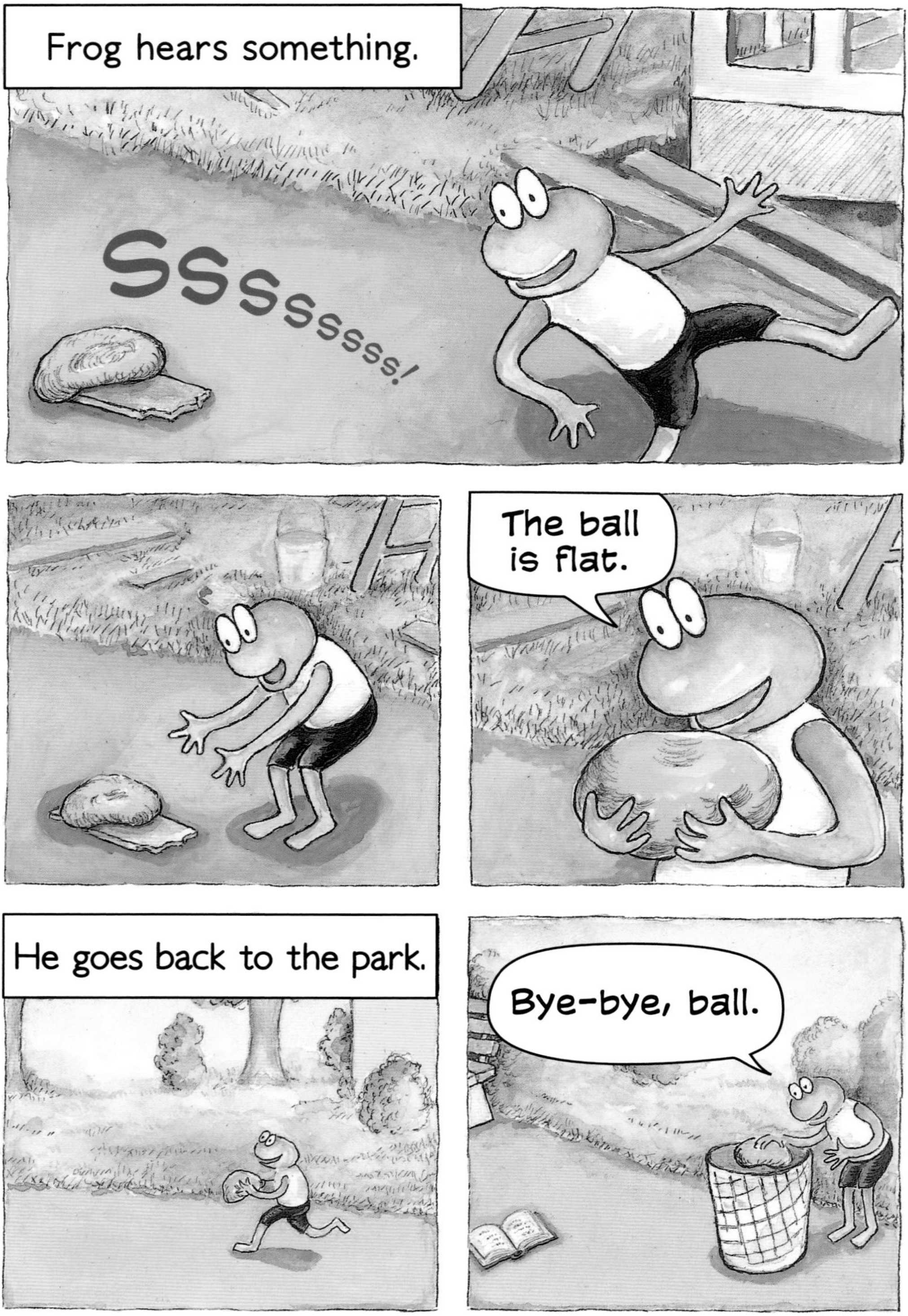
Frog hears something.
Sssssssss!
The ball is flat.
He goes back to the park.
Bye-bye, ball.

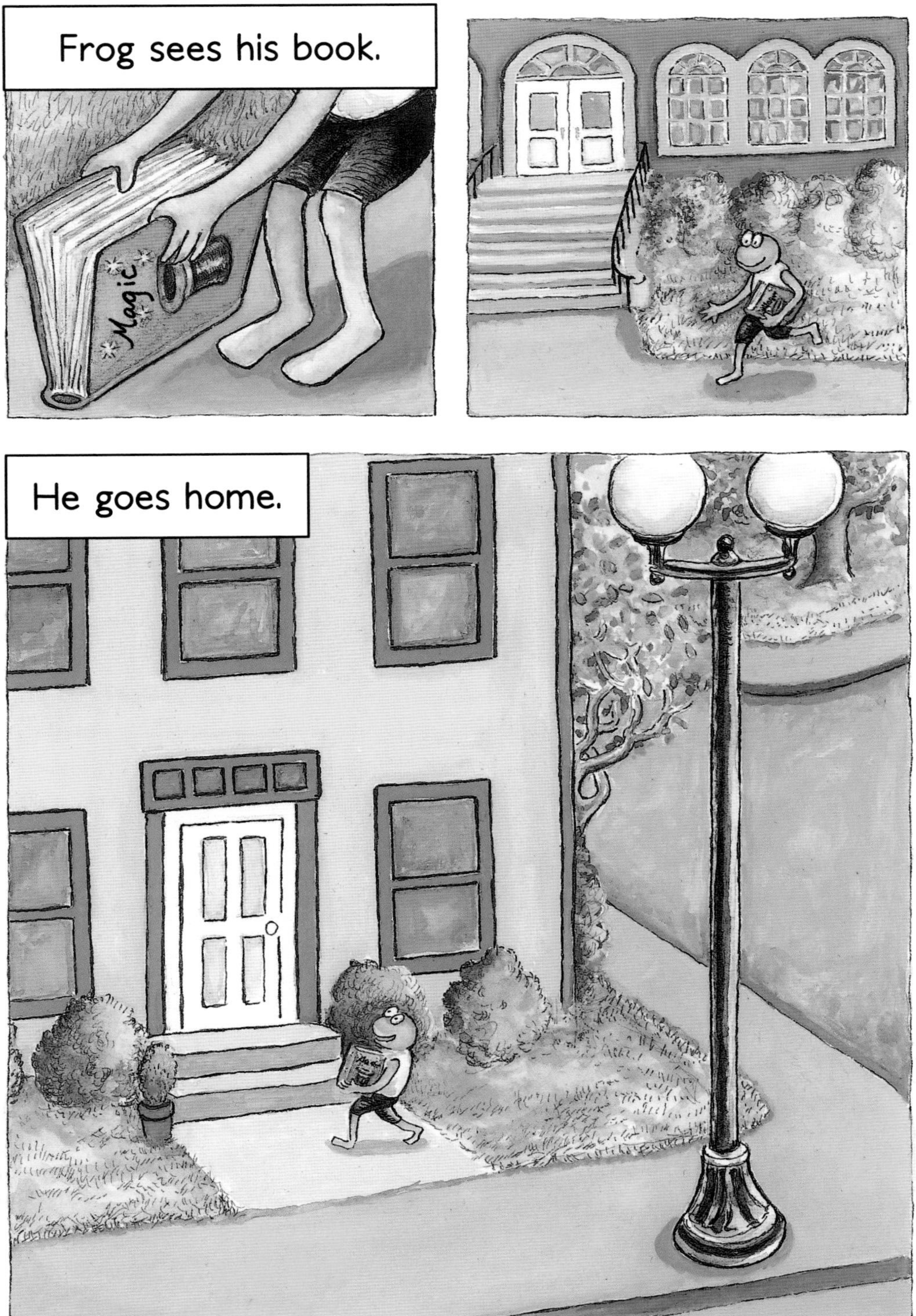
Frog sees his book.
Magic
He goes home.

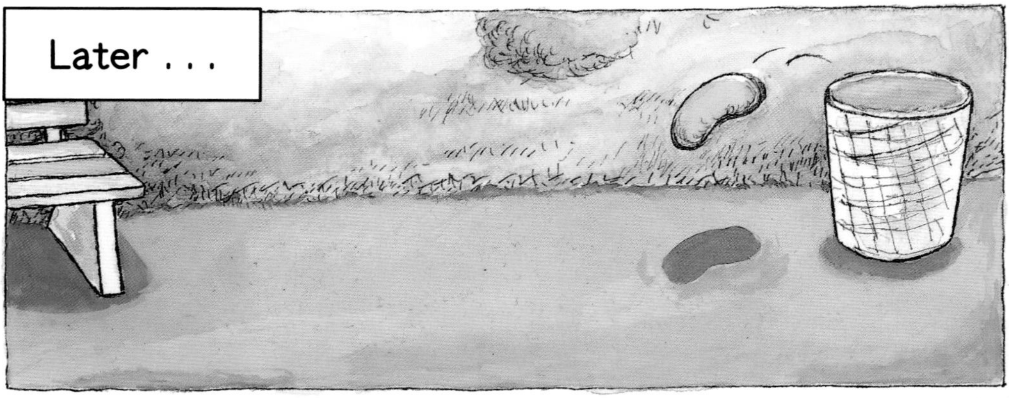
Later . . .

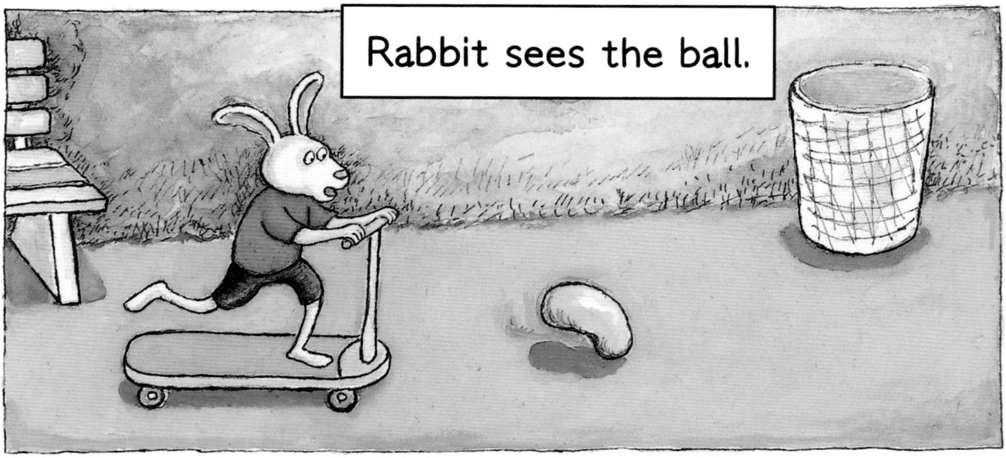
Rabbit sees the ball.

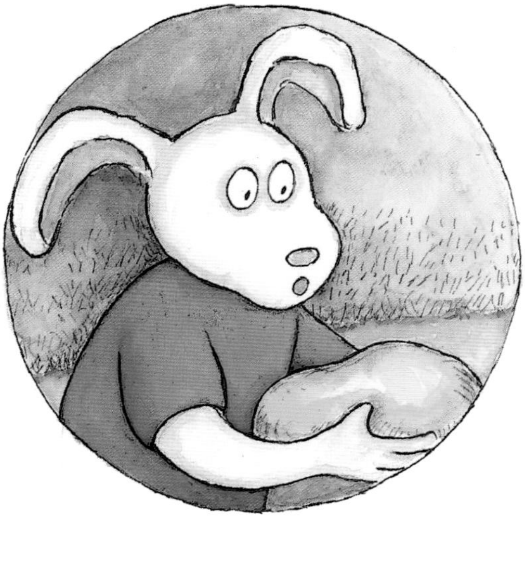

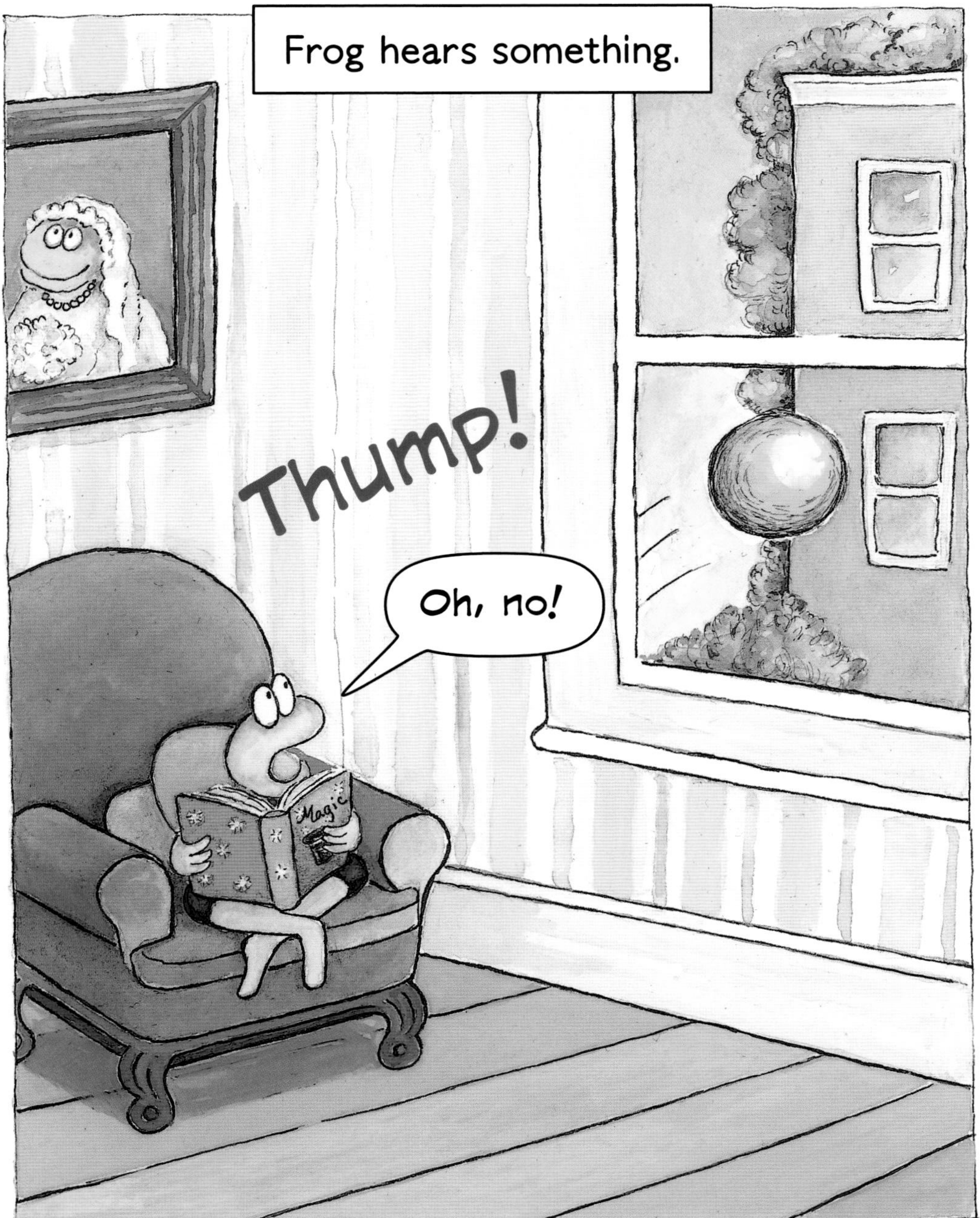
Frog hears something.
Thump!
Oh, no!
Magic

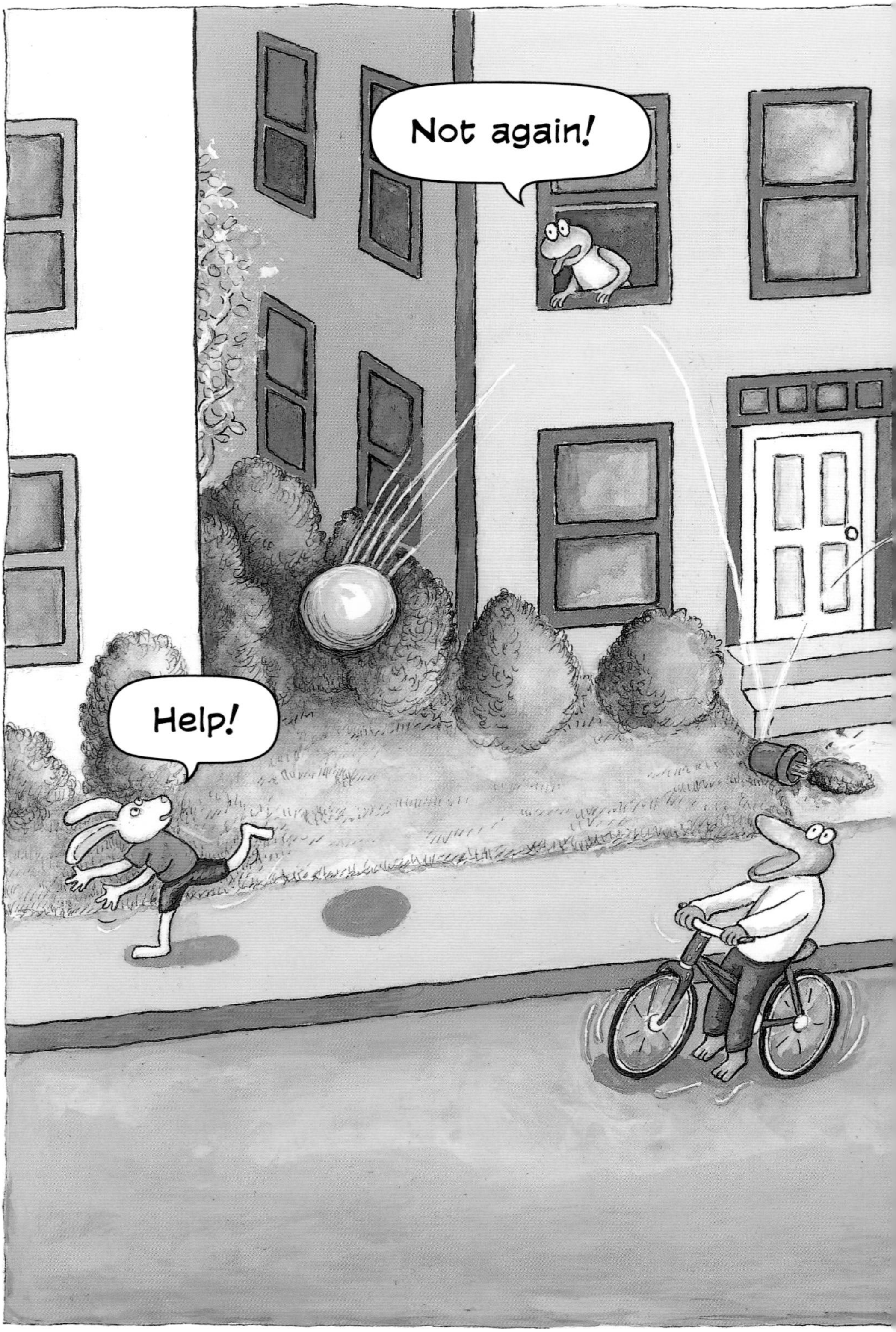
Not again!
Help!

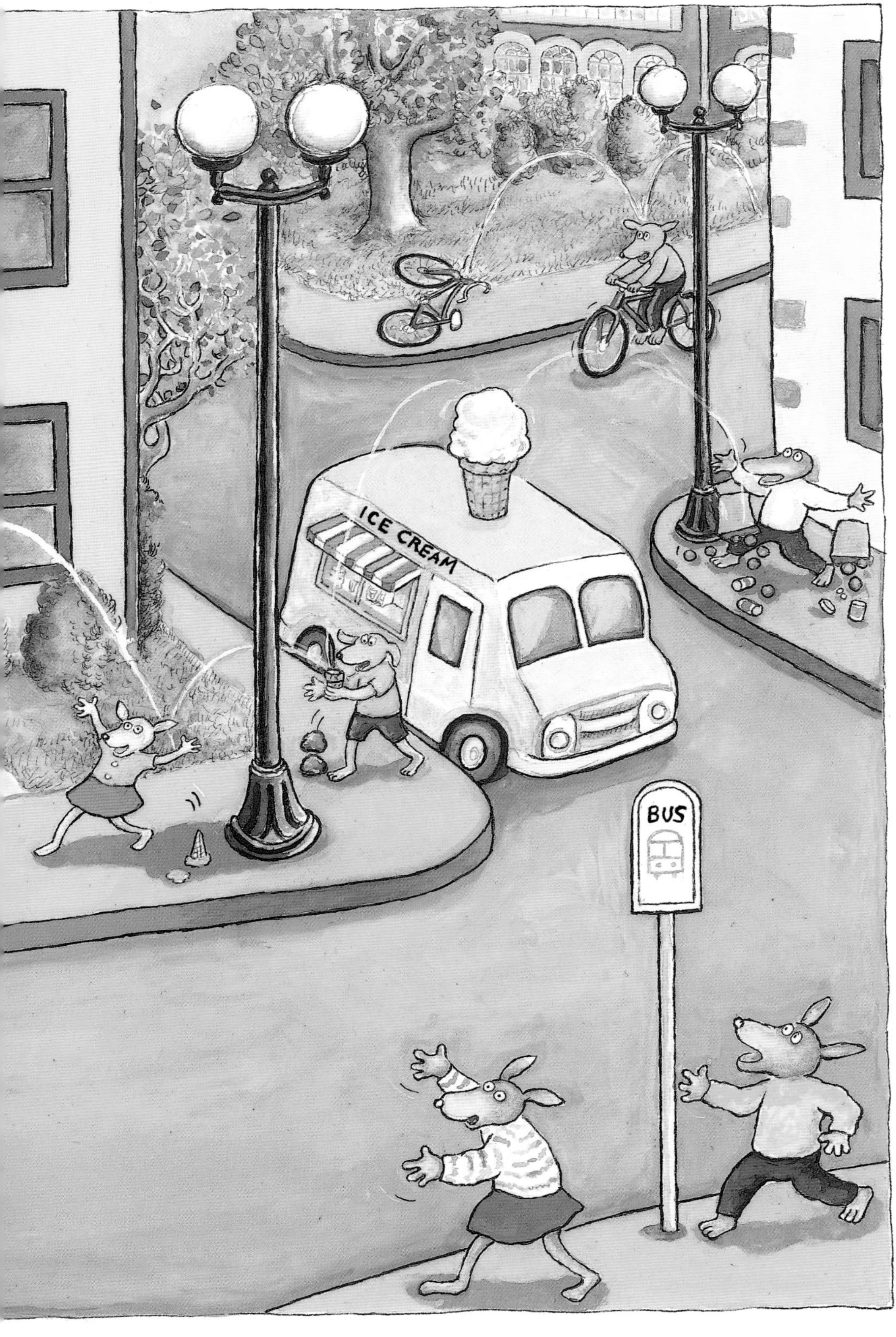
ICE CREAM
BUS

To my editor, Mary Cash, with much gratitude

I LIKE TO READ is a registered trademark of Holiday House Publishing, Inc.
Copyright © 2021 by Kathy Caple
All Rights Reserved
HOLIDAY HOUSE is registered in the U.S. Patent and Trademark Office.
Printed and bound in April 2021 at Leo Paper, Heshan, China.
The artwork was created on Arches 140 lb hot pressed watercolor paper, using Micron and Copic Multiliner
pens for inking, and painted with Winsor & Newton watercolors and gouache.
www.holidayhouse.com
First Edition
1 3 5 7 9 10 8 6 4 2

Library of Congress Cataloging-in-Publication Data

Names: Caple, Kathy, author, illustrator.
Title: Frog and ball / Kathy Caple.
Description: First edition. | New York : Holiday House, [2021] | Audience:
Ages 4-8. | Audience: Grades K-1. | Summary: When frog tries to fix a
flat ball with a magic spell, he accidentally brings it to life—and has
to flee for his life, pursued by the ball.
Identifiers: LCCN 2019029391 | ISBN 9780823443413 (hardcover)
Subjects: LCSH: Frogs—Comic books, strips, etc. | Frogs—Juvenile fiction.
| Balls (Sporting goods)—Comic books, strips, etc. | Balls (Sporting
goods)—Juvenile fiction. | Magic—Comic books, strips, etc.
Magic—Juvenile fiction. | Graphic novels. | Humorous stories. | CYAC:
Graphic novels. | Humorous stories. | Frogs—Fiction. | Balls (Sporting
goods)—Fiction. | Magic—Fiction. | LCGFT: Graphic novels. | Humorous fiction.
Classification: LCC PZ7.7.C364 Fr 2020 | DDC 741.5/973—dc23
LC record available at https://lccn.loc.gov/2019029391
ISBN: 978-0-8234-4341-3 (hardcover)
ISBN: 978-0-8234-4933-0 (paperback)

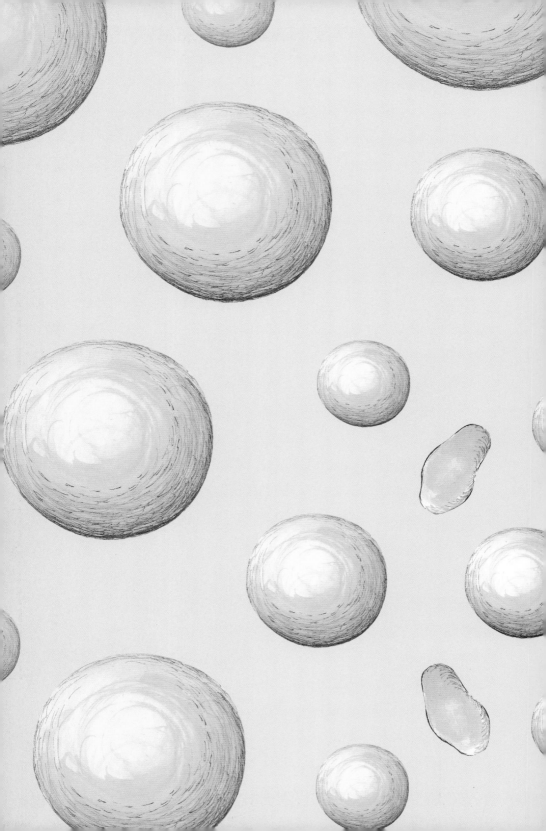